# Sweet William

## RICHMAL CROMPTON

Illustrated by Thomas Henry

### M
MACMILLAN CHILDREN'S BOOKS

First published 1936

First published in this edition 1986 by

MACMILLAN CHILDREN'S BOOKS
A division of Macmillan Publishers Limited
London and Basingstoke
Associated companies throughout the world

British Library Cataloguing in Publication Data
Crompton, Richmal
Sweet William.
Rn: Richmal Crompton Lamburn   I. Title
823'912[J]   PZ7

ISBN 0–333–41818–2
ISBN 0–333–41820–4 Pbk

Phototypeset by Wyvern Typesetting Ltd, Bristol
Printed in Great Britain by Cox & Wyman Ltd

# Contents

# An invitation from William

*Join my club and becum a noutlaw*
*William Brown*

# You can join the Outlaws Club!
You will receive
## * a special Outlaws wallet containing
your own Outlaws badge
the Club Rules
and
a letter from William giving you the secret password

To join the Club send a letter with your name and address written in block
capitals telling us you want to join the Outlaws, and a postal order for
45p, to

The Outlaws Club
PO Box No 702
London
SW20 8SZ

You must live in the United Kingdom or the Republic of Ireland in order
to join.

# Chapter 1

# William and the Wonderful Present

William strolled through the village, his hands in his pockets, his lips pursed up to emit a loud untuneful whistle.

He had a whole half-holiday at his disposal, and was inclined to let Fate take it and do what she would with it. He was in the mood for adventure, and he felt that adventure might be waiting for him round any corner. If, however, no adventure waited for him, he meant to go and spend the afternoon in the grounds of the Hall. The Botts, who owned the Hall, had gone away, leaving in charge a caretaker who was partially deaf, partially blind, and more than partially slow-witted. Empty houses always had a strong fascination for William. He felt that anything might happen in them. And, even if it didn't, one could pretend that they were enemies' fortresses or castles, or even pirate ships or desert islands. In any case, there was little danger on this occasion of the fun's being spoilt by gardeners, as it so often was, because Mrs. Bott had given all her gardeners, except one, a week's holiday, and that one spent most of his time dozing in a chair in the green-house.

As he walked along the road, his thoughts went to

Robert, his elder brother, whom he had left at home in a state of extreme nervous tension. For Robert was, not for the first time, in love. The beloved, who rejoiced in the name of Dahlia Macnamara, was a recent addition to the neighbourhood. Her family had only moved to the village last month. They were smart, sophisticated, and obviously monied, and, so far, Dahlia had given Robert little encouragement. She had, however, invited him to her birthday party to-day, and he had been to Hadley yesterday evening to buy her a present. It was the present that was worrying him. He was afraid that it wasn't good enough. He had noticed that all her things looked expensive, and this present didn't look expensive, for the simple reason that he'd only had three and six left from his allowance to spend on it. He'd bought her a necklace of green and red stones. It had looked very effective in the shop, but it looked less effective now every time he took it out of its box to inspect it. He was beginning, indeed, to have a horrible suspicion that it looked common. The thought that she might find it so and judge him accordingly, turned him hot and cold all over, and he had a wild temptation to sell his motor bike in order to buy her something really splendid. Common sense, however, prevailed. The saner part of him realised that girls may come and girls may go, but a motor bike remains a motor bike. He was, however, desperately worried about the necklace. He kept taking it out of its box and asking his mother what she thought of it.

"I think it's very nice, dear," his mother kept saying. "I'm sure she'll be very pleased with it."

The reassurance, instead of reassuring him, only increased his nervous tension.

"You don't understand," he said wildly. "She's the

most marvellous person in the world. And she's used to the most marvellous things. I mean, really expensive things.''

"Well, if you don't think she'll like it, don't give it her, dear.''

"But, Mother, I must give her something, and it's the only thing I've got.''

"Then give it her, dear. I think it's very nice, and I'm sure she'll be very pleased with it.''

The conversation went round and round in a circle like this, Mrs. Brown remaining placid and unmoved, Robert growing wilder and wilder.

William shook his head sadly at the memory. He could never understand how Robert, with all the world before him, could waste time and thought on such unimportant creatures as girls.

He had reached the gate of the Hall now, and as no other adventure had presented itself to him, he entered, keeping a cautious look-out for the gardener in case he should be taking a stroll in the neighbourhood of the house.

A few minutes' inspection satisfied him that the gardener was, as usual, dozing in the greenhouse, and that the caretaker, also as usual, was dozing in front of the kitchen fire. He crept round the house stealthily, peeping into each window. Suddenly he stopped open-mouthed with amazement. A tall thin man with red hair was standing in the shadow of some shrubs, looking in at the library window.

"Hello,'' said the man easily. "What are you doing here?''

"Well, what are you?'' countered William.

"Me?'' the man smiled. "Oh, I've just come down from Scotland Yard. There've been a lot of burglaries in

"WHAT ARE *YOU* DOING?" WILLIAM RETORTED.
"ME?" THE MAN ANSWERED. "OH, I'VE JUST COME DOWN
FROM SCOTLAND YARD."

empty houses lately, so I'm just keeping an eye on this
one."

William gasped and his eyes gleamed excitedly. A real
Scotland Yard detective. It seemed almost too good to

be true. He gazed with eager adoration at the red-haired man.

"I say—do tell me——" he was beginning, when he noticed another man approaching furtively through the shrubbery—a small shabby man with a few days' growth of beard on his chin. He slunk away again at a sign from William's companion.

"Who's he?" said William with interest.

"He's a detective, too," said the man. "He's very high up in Scotland Yard."

"Why is his face like that?" enquired William. "I mean, why doesn't he shave?"

"Oh, that!" said the man. "He's growing a beard. You see, he's such a very famous detective that most of the criminals have got to know him, so he's starting growing a beard now as a disguise."

"I see," said William, completely satisfied by the explanation.

"The people who live here are all away, aren't they?" said the man.

"Yes," said William, intensely flattered at being thus appealed to for information by Scotland Yard. "There's only the ole caretaker an' she's not much good 'cause she sleeps all day long an' anyway she's as deaf as a post."

"Good!" said the man. "I mean, bad! No wonder these empty houses are so often burgled. I must make a report of that to Scotland Yard. And what about the gardeners?"

"There's only one working here while they're away," said William importantly, "an' he's in the greenhouse right at the other end of the garden. He stays there most of the time. He's got a chair down there."

"Very bad, indeed," said the man, shaking his head.

"Dear, dear! Why aren't people more careful when they go away from home? Well"—he looked at William—"you'd like to go off and play with your friends now, I've no doubt."

But it turned out that William had no desire at all to go off and play with his friends. It was the first time he'd met a detective from Scotland Yard, and he meant to make the most of it.

"No," he said. "I'll stay'n' help. Honest, I bet I can help all right."

At this point the detective who was growing a beard came out of the shrubbery again and looked at William with increased disfavour.

"Well, are we goin' to get a move on or aren't we?" he said to his friend in a husky whisper.

His friend gave him a long slow wink.

"I've just been telling this young gent about us being detectives from Scotland Yard, keeping an eye on empty houses," he said. "Disgraceful, the carelessness of some of these people, isn't it?"

"Aw . . . come on," muttered the other sullenly. "'Ow much more time are you going to waste?"

The red-haired one smiled at William.

"My friend wants to get on with the job," he said. "We had instructions to take a look round inside as well as out, and make sure that no one's stolen anything while these people have been away."

"Can I come, too?" said William eagerly. "I'm goin' to be a detective when I grow up. I've practised a lot, I have, honest. I can help, findin' clues an' things."

The red-haired man looked at him thoughtfully.

"Yes," he said at last, "I think you might come too." He winked again at the other. "Our young friend will be safer with us in the circumstances, I think."

"Oh, I'll be safe all right," William assured him earnestly. "Don't you worry about me. I can take care of myself. If there is any criminals about I bet it's them won't be safe, not me, once I start on 'em."

"Good!" said the man.

The other growled.

The first took out his penknife, pushed it between the sash frames of the library window, then cautiously raised the lower one.

"Dear, dear!" he said again sadly. "Just think how easily a burglar might have done that!" He turned to the other. "Make a note of that in your report to the Yard."

The other growled again.

The three of them climbed through the window into the library. William was in the seventh heaven of delight. He could hardly believe it. He was helping two real live Scotland Yard detectives. He'd remember this all the rest of his life. Cautiously the three crept upstairs. The red-haired one held a short whispered conversation with his friend, then the bearded one went into Mrs. Bott's bedroom, and the other drew William into the spare bedroom.

"We'll see if anything's been tampered with here first," he said. "I'll look through these drawers. You look round and see if you can see any finger-prints."

William went to the window and gave a gasp of excitement. The village policeman was walking up the drive.

"Gosh!" he said. "There's the policeman. I say, I'll run down and tell him you're here, shall I?"

"No," said the man. "No, I wouldn't do that. You see," he went on after a slight pause, "that's the very policeman the Yard suspects of burgling empty houses while the owners are away."

"*Crumbs!*" breathed William aghast.

"That's really why we're here," went on the man in a confidential whisper. "And, of course, if he finds out we're here, he'll know the game's up and run away. We want to catch him in the act. Don't let him see you."

William hastily withdrew into the shadow of the curtain. He was intoxicated with rapture. This was the very stuff of which detective novels were made. And it was real. And he was in the thick of it. He was working with Scotland Yard to bring a famous criminal to justice.

"Can you see what he's doing now?" said the man.

William peeped cautiously out.

"He's coming to the front door," he said. "No, he isn't. He's standing looking up at this window. He can't see me, but he's looking up at it."

The man with the beard came in. He held a box in his hands.

"Got 'em all right," he said. "Come on."

"Can't," said the first succinctly. "The cop's here."

"Blimey!"

William ascribed the bearded man's obvious emotion to triumph at having got the criminal at last within his grasp.

The two conferred together. Isolated, uncomprehended phrases reached William. "Not risk it . . . " "with the stuff on us . . . " "ten years. . . . "

The red-haired man looked round the room. On a table near the window was some brown paper and a bit of string. He hastily made the box into a parcel and handed it to William.

"I've put in this box," he said, "all the clues we've found that will incriminate the policeman. There's a button from his uniform that he left behind in a house he'd burgled, and his finger-prints, and various other things we've found. But we want to slip away from here without him knowing anything about it. Once we rouse his suspicions, he'll escape, and we'll never catch him. So we don't want him to find us with that box on us. Now we'll give it to you to take care of for us till we've got out of the house, and then meet us with it, say, in an hour's time from now. Where can we meet, where no one's likely to see us?"

"Coombe Wood," said William excitedly. "Jus' where the field path goes into it. There's a big holly bush there."

"Good!" said the man. "Keep it all dead secret, mind. Don't say a word to anyone, and don't let a soul see the box. Then we'll get that policeman all right, and Scotland Yard will reward you."

"Gosh!" said William ecstatically. "You bet I will."

"We're going now. When we've gone you must hide up here a bit, then get out without anyone seeing you, and be at that place you said in an hour's time. And, if we're not there, by any chance, hide the parcel in the bush and we'll come back an' get it later. See?"

"Crumbs, yes!" said William and added excitedly, "I say, d'you think they'll make me a detective?"

"I've no doubt of it at all."

"A high-up one?"

"Certainly. . . . Where's the policeman now?"

William peeped cautiously out of the window.

"He's goin' round to the front door."

"Can he see this window?"

"No, he's gone now."

"Well, don't forget. Come on, Bill."

He opened the window, and the two men swarmed lightly down a drain-pipe that ran conveniently near. As soon as they reached the ground the policeman suddenly appeared, and the three of them set off at a brisk run, the policeman pursuing the two detectives.

William remained in hiding for about ten minutes. He could still hardly believe that this wonderful thing had happened to him. But it had. There was the brown paper parcel to prove it. The house remained silent. There were no further signs of policeman or detectives. He made his way quietly downstairs, and, finding the library window still open, climbed out of it and went home.

His mother came from the dining-room as he entered the hall. Hastily he slipped the brown paper parcel behind a raincoat that hung over the hall table. He mustn't let his mother find out about it. The detectives had insisted on the need of secrecy, and William, who felt himself now to be practically an official of Scotland Yard, was determined to uphold all its traditions.

"William, what a sight you look!" Mrs. Brown greeted him. "Go upstairs and wash at once."

He went upstairs to wash, then came down to the dining-room and set to work upon the thick slices of bread and jam with which he was wont to dull the keen edge of his appetite.

Next, Robert came downstairs, spick and span and pale and intense-looking. He carried a small brown paper parcel in his hands. Slipping it on the hall table—for he didn't want that kid, William, making fool remarks about it—he went into the dining-room, where Mrs. Brown, having had her tea, sat by the window knitting.

"You look very nice, dear," she said.

"I don't," snapped Robert, who was still in an acute state of nerves. "I wonder if I'd better start now. I don't want to be too early."

"Of course not, dear."

"On the other hand, I don't want to be too late."

"Of course not, dear."

"I don't know whether to take her that present or not," he went on.

"Who? What present?" said William, his mouth full of bread and jam.

"Shut up and mind your own business," said Robert savagely, glad of an opportunity of venting his irritation on someone.

"All right. Keep your hair on," muttered William, returning to his bread and jam.

"I think it's a very nice present, dear," said Mrs. Brown placidly.

"Do you really?" said Robert. "I mean—well, you know what she is. And, after all—well, three-and-six. I expect she'll have the most *marvellous* things."

"Anyway, dear," Mrs. Brown consoled him, "it's not the value of the gift that matters, it's the thought."

"But I don't want it to be that sort of a present," burst out the exasperated Robert.

"What sort, dear?"

"The sort you have to think that it's the thought that matters."

"But it is, dear. I mean it *does*. . . . It's a very nice necklace. For three-and-six, I mean. And, anyway, three-and-six is enough to spend on anyone. It's the thought that——"

Robert flung himself from the room with a furious exclamation and stood at the front door looking up at the sky. It was darkening for a storm. He didn't want to arrive at *her* birthday party wet through. He took his raincoat from its peg, and, snatching up the brown paper parcel, below it, strode out with set, tense face, slamming the door violently behind him.

William finished his tea and went out into the hall. No one was about. His mother was still knitting by the dining-room window. He took the brown paper parcel from the hatstand, put it under his jacket, and made his way quickly to Coombe Wood. It was just an hour since he'd parted from the two detectives. No one was there. He waited till supper-time, then, as still no one had come, thrust the parcel into the bush, and went home to bed. He felt slightly worried by the non-appearance of the detectives, but thought that, perhaps, they had to wait till nightfall, and that they would come back under cover of darkness. After all, they had told him to leave it in the bush, so it was probably all right. They would, of course, have to be very careful. The policeman must have found out by now that they were on his track, and would be desperate.

Robert came home soon after William had had his supper. Gone was all his moodiness and irritation. He was elated. He walked on air. Dahlia had received him coldly. She had received his present coldly. She obviously thought him no great shakes, and would have enjoyed her birthday just as well without either him or his present. She took the box carelessly and put it away without opening it, then continued to ignore him and to make herself pleasant to a gilded youth who had come down from London for the day. Robert wandered about moodily, wishing he hadn't bought the wretched necklace, wishing he hadn't come to the wretched birthday party, wishing he'd never been born. . . .

Then she disappeared, taking the unopened present with her, and, just as Robert was wondering whether to sneak off home, she returned and approached him with a smile so radiant that he simply couldn't believe that it could be really meant for him. He thought it must be

"IT'S MARVELLOUS!" SHE SAID. "IT'S LOVELY! I CAN'T THINK
WHAT IT MUST HAVE COST YOU."

meant for the gilded youth. But it wasn't. It was meant
for him. She thanked him for his present with an
effusiveness that took his breath away.

"It's *lovely*!" she said. "It's simply *marvellous*!"

"Oh, it's nothing," said Robert modestly. "Just a
very ordinary necklace. . . ."

"Ordinary!" she echoed. "It's *marvellous*. I can't

think what it must have cost you. Or, perhaps, it's something that was in your family. I mean, something that was left you or something."

"Oh, no," said Robert, trying to fight against the feeling that all this must be happening in a dream."Oh, no, it wasn't left me. I bought it."

"Well, I think it was wonderful of you. Wonderful! I'd no idea. . . . I think it's wonderful. You don't mind me not wearing it now, do you? It's too lovely to be worn with an ordinary tennis dress like this. Are you going to the Millers' dance on Wednesday?"

"Yes."

"I'll wear it then. I'll wear it with my new evening dress. Honestly, I've never seen anything so wonderful. I could hardly believe my eyes when I saw it. . . . "

"B-but it was nothing," stammered Robert. "Nothing at all. Just a cheap necklace."

"*Cheap!*" she echoed with a laugh. "I'm sure it wasn't *cheap*. Anyway, I can't tell you how grateful I am."

Robert was essentially honest, and it was on the tip of his tongue to tell her that it had cost three-and-six. He checked himself in time, however. Evidently it looked as if it cost more than three-and-six. It might even look as if it had cost seven-and-six. No need to undeceive her if she thought it had cost as much as seven-and-six. After all, it *was* a very nice necklace. His mother had said so. The more he thought of it, in the light of her glowing approval, the nicer it seemed. He couldn't think how he had ever thought it looked common.

"It will look simply *wonderful* with the dress I'm going to wear at the Millers' dance," she went on.

Taste, that was it, thought Robert. It wasn't a question of money. It was just a question of taste. He must have better taste than he'd realised.

"Will you dance with me at the Millers' dance?" he said daringly.

"Of *course*."

He dared further.

"Will you give me two?" he said.

"Three, if you like," she said fondly.

Through Robert's dizzy brain flashed the thought that, perhaps, he possessed sex appeal. He'd never even suspected it before. Certainly Dahlia's previous behaviour had not encouraged the idea, but, perhaps, it was the sort of sex appeal that took some time to get going. Once going, however, it certainly hustled.

The dream continued for the rest of the afternoon. Dahlia hung on his words and looks, snubbing the gilded youth so cruelly that even Robert was sorry for him. As she said good-bye to him, she murmured:

"Thank you again for your *wonderful* present. It's the most *wonderful* present I've ever had in my life."

Robert walked home, still in the dream. His feet didn't seem to touch the ground, because there didn't seem to be any ground to touch and he didn't seem to have any feet to touch it with.

William awoke early the next morning, and made his way at once to the wood. He was considerably disappointed to find the parcel still in the holly bush. He had expected that the detectives would have fetched it away in the night. He hoped nothing had happened to them. Suppose the policeman, knowing that the game was up, and feeling desperate, had killed them. . . . The fact that the parcel was still in the holly bush was almost a proof that this had happened. If the detectives had been alive, they would have come back to fetch it and take it to Scotland Yard. A feeling of great responsibility descended upon William. The duty of bringing the policeman to justice seemed now to devolve solely upon him. He went home to breakfast and was unusually silent throughout the meal. Once he said:

"Father, is there anythin' in the paper about two detectives bein' murdered?"

"No," said his father shortly, "and don't talk with your mouth full."

"Why? Have you murdered them?" said Robert genially.

Robert was in radiant good humour. The dream was still continuing. He had received a note from Dahlia, by the morning's post, asking him to go to tea there this afternoon. At first he couldn't believe it. He read it six or seven times, but the words continued to bear the same meaning. It was true. She actually asked him to go there to tea again this afternoon. The letter ended: "And I must tell you once more how much I love your *wonderful* present."

"No, I haven't," said William darkly, "but, if there have been, I bet I jolly well know who's done it."

"I suppose Scotland Yard confides in you?" said Robert.

William gave a meaning laugh. Robert little knew how true his words were!

After breakfast he went to school as usual. He was distrait throughout the morning and missed several pearls of sarcasm cast before him by the geography and science masters.

He was wondering how to bring the policeman to justice, if the box continued to remain in the holly bush. Suppose that the policeman knew of its existence, and was even now searching for it. . . . Suppose that he knew that he, William, was aware of his guilt. . . . He'd have as little compunction in putting him out of the way, as he'd had in putting the detectives out of the way (for William was beginning to feel certain that this was what had happened). He felt that he was, indeed, deeply involved in the tangled mesh of crime. He wondered whether to write direct to Scotland Yard and tell them the whole story, but he didn't know the address, and he felt that to ask the policeman for it would certainly arouse his suspicions, if, by any chance, they were not aroused already.

He returned home at lunch-time to find his family in a state of great excitement. Ethel had heard in the village that the policeman had discovered that there'd been a burglary at the Hall and had wired for the Botts to come home. William was aghast at this further proof of the villain's depravity. He'd robbed the place himself, of course, and was trying to make out that it had been done by burglars.

He wondered whether to give him a hint that he knew all, but he decided not to, as that might drive him to fling himself down from a cliff or shoot himself (in all the thrillers William had read the villain flung himself down from a cliff, or shot himself, on the last page), and, of course, he didn't want that.

He spent the whole of afternoon school debating on his next move. He took an hour to write an essay consisting of a line and a half. He spent half an hour over a single sum, in which he came to the conclusion that it would take four men three hundred years to mow a meadow of two square acres. He told the history master that Henry VI was killed at the battle of Waterloo. He endured the combined reproaches of the maths. and history masters with philosophical calm, stayed in for half an hour's detention, then walked quickly to

Coombe Wood. The box was still in the holly bush. There didn't seem much chance of the detectives' fetching it now, and, as the policeman, who was, presumably, searching for it, might come on it any moment, William decided to take charge of it himself. He slipped it under his jacket and set off towards the Hall. He had decided to tell Mrs. Bott the whole story, and ask her to get into touch at once with Scotland Yard. Grown-ups presumably had means of getting into touch with Scotland Yard that he knew nothing of.

He walked up to the door of the Hall and there met with his first set-back. The deaf caretaker, after informing him indignantly that she could hear as well as he could *and* better (not wishing to waste time, he'd bawled his question into her ear with undue violence), said that Mrs. Bott was not at home. She'd gone out to tea to Mrs. Macnamara's. And would he please take his dirty boots off her clean doorstep and—— William walked quickly away without staying to hear more. He hurried down the road towards Mrs. Macnamara's. On the way he met the village policeman—an innocent-looking youth, whose chief ambition in life was to grow a moustache. (A faint down on his upper lip was all he had so far been able to achieve, despite the application of hair restorer in various forms.) William gave him a long, slow, accusing look.

"Now then," said the policeman, forestalling any remark that William might make, "none of your sauce!"

He had had many skirmishes with William in the past, and had often chased him out of the property of various local land-owners, but he bore him no ill will. In fact, he secretly welcomed the diversion that William brought into his otherwise dull life. The burglary at the Hall, of course, was bringing a certain amount of diversion into it at present, but the policeman didn't really think that anything was going to come of it. The two thieves had got away, and nothing had been heard of them since. In any case it wouldn't accrue to his credit now, even if the thieves were caught.

William walked on, thinking how unlike a villain the policeman looked. But, on second thoughts, he didn't really look unlike a villain. In all the detective stories William had read, it was the person whom you'd least suspect who turned out to have done it. The policeman was, therefore, a typical villain. One might almost have guessed he'd done it, even if one hadn't known. As he drew near Mrs. Macnamara's house he slackened his pace. He'd better not tell Mrs. Bott in front of the Macnamaras and whoever else happened to be present. He'd try to get her alone. It was terribly important that no one else should know. The policeman was quite capable of murdering them all, before he flung himself down from a cliff or shot himself.

The maid who answered the door said that Mrs. Macnamara was in. She looked at William with the disfavour with which all domestics were wont to regard him, and admitted him grudgingly, ordering him to wipe his boots, and, for goodness' sake, try to get some of that mud off.

William obeyed, maintaining a dignified silence, and was ushered into the drawing-room. There sat Mrs. Macnamara, Mrs. Bott, Dahlia and—to William's surprise—Robert. Dahlia was wearing a navy blue satin dress and a magnificent string of pearls, to which she kept making cryptic allusion that baffled and bewildered Robert.

"Don't you think they look *wonderful*?" she said.

He agreed vaguely that they did.

"Simply *marvellous*. I can't tell you how I love them." She patted and rearranged the pearls. "They've got such a perfectly wonderful sheen, haven't they?"

"Er—yes."

"By the way, I've promised to go over to the Gregsons' dance at Marleigh next month. Will you come as my partner? *Do*. I really don't want to go if you won't come. You will come, won't you?"

He agreed rapturously, and came to the conclusion once more that he must possess sex appeal in a most concentrated and magnetic form. Funny that he'd never suspected it before.

It was upon this peaceful scene that William intruded. Mrs. Macnamara, who was gossiping in a desultory fashion with Mrs. Bott at the other end of the room, looked at him with a vague smile. Mrs. Macnamara was a massive jewel-bedecked mountain of vagueness. A boy had arrived. He must be fed. It never even occurred to her to wonder why he had arrived.

"Sit down and have something to eat, dear," she said, waving him towards the cake stand, on which reposed a large chocolate iced cake.

William, looking at the iced cake, realised that he was hungry, and that it was tea-time. Everything, of course, in its due time and place. There is a time to eat, and a time to bring criminals to justice. This was the time to eat. There was, after all, no immediate hurry about bringing criminals to justice. The best thing to do would be to stay here till Mrs. Bott went home, then go with her and tell her the whole story on the way. The others had finished tea, so William settled himself down by the cake stand and set to work on the chocolate cake. Desultory scraps of the others' conversation reached him. Mrs. Bott, of course, was talking about the burglary.

"I'm not quite sure whether anything's gone but the pearls," she was saying. "It's difficult to remember just what one has. I never had much of a memory, and Botty's (Mrs. Bott always referred to her husband as Botty) abroad. But the pearls have been stolen all right. Kept trying to persuade me, Botty did, to put them in the bank before we went away, and I meant to, too, but, somehow, it slipped my mind. Anyway, I thought they'd be all right in the safe. Shows one never knows, doesn't it? Clever men, these criminals. That nice young policeman did his best to catch them, but they were one too many for him."

William could not resist a sardonic snort over his chocolate cake.

"You'll be at the tennis club to-morrow, won't you?" Dahlia was saying fondly to Robert.

"Yes, *rather*!" said Robert, giving her a languishing smile, then, hearing William's snort, turning to glare at him. It seemed as if one simply couldn't go anywhere where that wretched kid didn't turn up. He'd arrived here from nowhere at all, for no reason at all, and sat wolfing cake as if he hadn't been fed for weeks. How could one do justice to oneself, in the eyes of the most wonderful girl in the world, with that kid sitting there listening to every word one said and as likely as not to bring it all out next time one had a row with him?

"They were very valuable pearls, I suppose?" Mrs. Macnamara was saying.

"Oh, yes," said Mrs. Bott. "Botty gave them to me the year we came here. Very valuable indeed. Of course, they're insured. They were beautiful pearls. They . . . " Her eyes fell suddenly on the string of pearls with which Dahlia was elegantly toying. She stopped abruptly, and stared at them as if fascinated. "They were—very like

MRS. BOTT EXAMINED THE NECKLACE AND HER FACE GREW
PALER AND PALER. SHE TRIED TO SPEAK, BUT NO WORDS
WOULD COME.

the pearls your daughter's wearing," she said in a faint
voice.

Mrs. Macnamara laughed.

"Oh, those!" she said. "They're not real, of course.
It's simply marvellous how they get up this false jewelry
nowadays."

Dahlia examined the beads complacently.

"They're lovely, anyway," she said. "I shouldn't be

WILLIAM'S WHOLE ATTENTION WAS STILL CONCENTRATED ON
THE CHOCOLATE CAKE.

surprised if *someone*"—she smiled coyly at the
bewildered Robert from under her lashes— "paid quite
a lot for them."

"May I—may I see them, dear?" said Mrs. Bott, still
in that faint far-away voice.

"Certainly," said Dahlia again, sending the ecstatic,
but bewildered, Robert another arch and meaning

smile, as she slipped them off and handed them to Mrs. Bott. Mrs. Bott examined them, her face growing paler and paler. There couldn't be any mistake. There were the two of irregular size near the end. There was the one with the slight flaw. There was the brilliant missing from the clasp. She raised her face and tried to speak, but no words would come. The others gaped at her in astonishment, all except William, whose whole attention was still concentrated on the chocolate cake and who continued to munch unmoved.

Just then the door was flung open, and the village policeman entered, accompanied by another man, who obviously represented authority.

" 'Scuse me, ladies," he said to the assembly, "but I was told that Mrs. Bott was here, and I've something very important to say to her. No, don't move, ladies. It won't take a minute, and then I won't trouble you any more. We've got those two men that broke open your house, madam—tall man with red hair, and a little dark one. We've been after them for months. I'm afraid I can't tell you where your pearls are. There's no trace of 'em."

Mrs. Bott found her voice at last.

"These are my pearls," she said, waving the string aloft.

"*Nonsense!*" said Dahlia, snatching at them indignantly. "They're mine. They're a present. I had them yesterday. They're not real pearls at all."

"Excuse me, madam," said Authority. He took the pearls and examined them with an expert's eye. "I should say, madam, that they were real pearls, and extremely valuable ones at that."

Mrs. Bott gulped.

"They're my pearls," she said again hysterically. "I'd

know them anywhere. Look! Those two aren't quite the right size. Look at the clasp, and you'll see that there's a stone out. Botty kept saying I ought to have it put in again. Oh, dear! Oh, dear! What can it all mean?"

"I don't know what you're talking about," said Dahlia icily. "Those beads were a present from this gentleman." She waved a shapely hand at Robert. "He gave me them yesterday."

It was Robert's turn to look wild.

"I didn't," he said. "I swear I didn't. I never saw them till this minute."

"Oo!" gasped Dahlia. "How can you tell such *lies*?"

Mrs. Macnamara joined the fray.

"The pearls were certainly a present from this young gentleman," she said. "I was there when my daughter opened the parcel. I saw him give it her, and I saw her open it. I'd swear to it in any court of law."

"So would I," said Dahlia, glaring at the unhappy Robert.

"Oh, dear, oh, dear!" moaned Mrs. Bott. "Such a nice young man and of such a good family!"

"I've never seen them in my life till this minute," said Robert again, in a strangled voice. They were all staring at him accusingly. He looked the picture of guilt.

"I'm afraid you'll have to explain how these pearls came into your possession, young man," said Authority, "and I caution you that anything you say may be used as evidence against you."

Robert's mouth opened and shut like the mouth of an expiring fish. Incoherent phrases came from it. "I never . . . I didn't. . . . I didn't . . . I never. . . . "

"Oh, dear, oh, dear!" moaned Mrs. Bott. "What *will* his mother say?"

William, swallowing the last remnants of the choc-

olate cake, had been wondering at what point he should
intervene. He decided that the point had now arrived.
He rose to his feet, sending a plentiful sprinkling of
chocolate cake crumbs on to the carpet.

"Robert didn't steal them," he said. "I know who
stole them."

"Who did, then?" demanded Authority.

William extended an accusing hand to the young
policeman. "*He* did," he said firmly. "And I've got
proof he did."

Robert ceased to be the focus of attention, and the
limelight passed to William, who stood sternly confront-
ing the amazed young man in the policeman's uniform.

"Let's have your proof," said Authority grimly.

"I've got it all right," said William equally grimly.
"Those two men—the one with red hair and the other—
aren't thieves at all. They're detectives from Scotland
Yard, an' they were after this policeman 'cause they
knew that he does burglaries in empty houses, an' it was
him that burgled the Hall, only he put it on to them an'
he's probably got them kidnapped somewhere in an
empty house or killed or——"

"That's enough of that rubbish," snapped Authority.

"It's not rubbish," said William, bringing out his
brown paper parcel, "and you'll find *proof* in here.
There's his finger-prints they found on stolen things, an'
a button off his uniform, what he left in one of the houses
he was burgling, and a lot of other proofs. You open it,
that's all. An' take care he doesn't throw himself from a
cliff or anything sudden."

Authority took the box, opened it and drew out a
cheap-looking necklace of red and green glass beads.

"It's my present," gasped Robert to Dahlia. "It's the
present I gave you."

"Me?" said Dahlia coldly.

"Yes. I gave it you. You said you liked it. You kept saying you liked it."

"*Me?*" said Dahlia again. "*Liked* it? *That* thing? I've never seen it before, and I hope I never see it again."

Authority had grasped William firmly by the ear.

"Now, young man," it said, "tell us the whole story from the beginning."

William told it. Only with the greatest difficulty was he persuaded that his detectives were not detectives, but a couple of well-known crooks. At long last, however, and very, very reluctantly, he was convinced. The whole affair was, in fact, cleared up to the satisfaction of everyone concerned, except Dahlia, who saw the pearl necklace, to which she had grown so deeply attached, returned to its original owner, and Robert, to whom Dahlia's manner had suddenly become so frigid that an iceberg would have been cordial in comparison. It appeared that she wouldn't have any dances to spare for him on Wednesday. It appeared that she didn't want him to take her to the Gregsons' dance. It appeared that she didn't want his red and green necklace. She told him so forcibly in so many words. It appeared, in fact, that Robert did not possess sex appeal, after all. . . .

\*     \*     \*

He and William walked home together sunk in gloomy thought.

"Well," said William, at last, "I don't think anyone's ever had such bad luck as me ever since the world began. It doesn't seem as if I'm ever goin' to get into Scotland Yard at this rate."

Robert said nothing.

His thoughts lay too deep for words.

# Chapter 2

# William and the Perfect Child

William and his Outlaws wandered slowly along the road. There were only two days of the summer holiday left and they were feeling aggrieved. The longer a holiday was, they decided, the more quickly it went, which didn't seem fair. William was feeling specially aggrieved. This afternoon he had been condemned to accompany his mother to a meeting at the Vicarage. It was the housemaid's afternoon off, and the cook said that she wouldn't be left in the house again with that young limb, not if they went down on their bended knees to her, she wouldn't. She'd pack up and go, she would, sooner. She was a good cook, so Mrs. Brown promised faithfully that the young limb should not be left with her, which meant that the young limb must accompany Mrs. Brown to the meeting of the Women's Guild at the Vicarage.

Even William had to admit that the last time he and the cook had been left together in the house events had taken an unfortunate turn. While the cook was upstairs he had carried out a few experiments with the gas oven, and the resultant explosion had nearly wrecked the kitchen. The cook had had hysterics, William had narrowly escaped with his life, the kitchen window and five shillings' worth of kitchen crockery had been broken. So that he was not altogether surprised— though he pretended to be—when his passionate protests were ignored and he was condemned to accompany his mother to the meeting of the Women's Guild. All the more reason, then, to make the most of the morning, and that was what William had decided to do. And yet, as generally happens in such cases, the morning was turning out unexpectedly flat. He and the Outlaws had played at Red Indians and Highwaymen and Lion Hunters, but all the accustomed zest seemed to be lacking from these games.

The thought of the beginning of term loomed over them like a black cloud, and the games petered out finally into an aimless wandering over the fields, interspersed with such remarks as: "I 'spect ole Stinks'll be worse than ever." "There isn't even goin' to be a new master to make things a bit excitin'." "Ole Markie's always worst at the beginnin' of term." "Ole Warbeck couldn't be worse than he was last term, but he's sure to be as bad." "While as for Monkey-Face . . . "

Slower and more dejected became their progress. Suddenly they stopped. A big grey horse was trotting up to them across the field. There was a slight apprehension at their hearts as it approached. It was massive and long-haired and wild-looking. But its intentions were obviously friendly. When William daringly put up a hand to pat and stroke it, it showed every sign of gratification. They all patted and stroked it. It nozzled them affectionately. They pulled up handfuls of grass and offered them to it. It ate them obligingly.

"I say," said William excitedly, "let's get it some sugar."

"I'll go an' get some," said Douglas. "Our house is nearest."

He ran off at full speed, and the other Outlaws continued to fraternise with their new acquaintance. As they went about the field selecting the more appetising patches of grass, the horse followed them trustingly. It even rested its head affectionately on William's shoulder, and a deep emotion stirred in his breast. This was what it must feel like to have a horse. A horse of one's own. . . . Douglas returned with the sugar. He had filled his pockets with it. The horse ate it with obvious enjoyment and gratitude. At last Henry said:

"Come on. We can't stop here for ever."

Very slowly they walked towards the gate that led into the next field. The horse followed them. William opened the gate to let his band through, and the horse passed through with them. William closed the gate. After all, he reasoned with himself, he couldn't help the horse coming through the gate. He couldn't have stopped it. Well, perhaps he could if he'd shut the gate quickly enough, but—anyway, there it was, following them across the next field as closely as if determined never to let them out of its sight again. An unfounded, but thrilling, pride of possession filled William's heart. His horse . . . *his* horse. . . . He opened the next gate and again the horse accompanied the band through it. Again William assured himself that it wasn't his fault. Well, not quite his fault. You couldn't stop a horse goin' where it wanted to, could you? It was a free country, wasn't it? The next gate led into the road. Down the road . . . past the Vicarage gates . . . in at another gate . . . across two more fields . . . till they reached the old barn . . . the horse following them all the time. At the old barn they stood and gazed fondly at their new pet. Then

Douglas handed round the remainder of the sugar, and they fed him in turn.

"Let's have a ride on him," said William.

They considered this suggestion for some moments in silence, then Douglas said: "We can't ride him without reins an' stuff."

Ginger broke in eagerly.

"There's some old harness in Farmer Jenks's barn. It's a bit raggy 'cause he never uses it, but I bet it'd do all right."

He was dispatched to Farmer Jenks's barn. Fate seemed to be on their side. The barn was deserted. Ginger cautiously "borrowed" a raggy saddle and bridle and returned triumphantly with it to the Outlaws. It took some little time to attach it to their steed. Not that the steed proved in any way refractory. It was, indeed, docility itself. Only the Outlaws were unskilled in the art of harnessing, and a less phlegmatic animal would have keenly resented their amateur efforts. When, finally, after many attempts, they had adjusted both saddle and bridle right way on and right way up, they stood and gazed at their handiwork in silent pride. A horse . . . saddled and bridled . . . their horse . . . their own horse. . . .

"Well," said William at last, in a voice he strove in vain to render airy and casual, "I'll jus' have a ride on him first, shall I?"

None of them challenged his right as leader to the first ride. Instead, they clustered round, hoisting him into the large and excessively shabby saddle. After several falls he found himself firmly established there. He took the reins, said "Gee up", and—the grey horse began obediently to lumber across the field. William's feelings were beyond description. No medieval knight in gleaming armour ever bestrode a gaily caparisoned horse with feelings of greater pride and arrogance. To William, in fact, both knight and horse would have seemed shabby in comparison with his mental picture of himself. A grubby little boy, perched on a saddle from which the stuffing was oozing at all points, on a large, clumsy, untended horse of one of the less distinguished breeds, with three other little boys trotting at its heels. . . . Not so did William see himself. He was a king, surrounded by his bodyguard. His thoroughbred pranced beneath him. The gold and jewels of his crown, the scarlet ermine of his cloak, made a noble splash of colour. Massed crowds cheered him on all sides as he rode along. . . . He was a general at the head of his army. His war horse pawed the air, snorted, neighed. His armour gleamed in the sun. The enemy fled in confusion before him.

It was with the greatest reluctance that he acceded to the others' clamorous requests for their "turn." Even when he had been finally dismounted by their combined force and Ginger had been established upon the saddle, William, plodding by his side, was not really plodding by his side. He was up there instead of Ginger . . . rallying his army . . . riding in triumph through cheering crowds . . . his gallant steed curvetting beneath him. It was his turn again. He tried to leap nimbly upon his charger, but fell down ignominiously and had to be hoisted up by the others as before. The fall had brought him down to earth, metaphorically as well as literally. He was no longer a king or a general on a thoroughbred. He was William on a horse. And that was, after all, almost as much a matter for pride as the other. Why should not he lead his Outlaws about the countryside on horseback? In imagination he saw himself doing this, saw the rival gangs, Hubert Lane's in particular, fleeing at his approach, saw himself arriving at school triumphantly on horseback, the admired of all beholders. He thought that he could probably find room in the school bicycle shed for his gallant grey during school hours.

There were certain practical difficulties to be over-come, of course. He could not keep the horse at home. In fact, he would prefer his parents to remain in ignorance of it altogether. The old barn would make quite a good stable, and they could keep the steed in the corner where the rain didn't come in. Tentatively he voiced these plans to the others. They were less enthusiastic about certain aspects of it than he was. The rôle of humble followers on foot did not altogether appeal to them.

"We all found it together," protested Ginger, "an' I don't see why we shouldn't have our turns tramplin' on our enemies an' suchlike."

"All right," said William at last, generously. "We'll have it a day each, but bags me have it when anything really important's goin' on."

They conceded that. William was, after all, their leader. It was Douglas who voiced the practical objection.

"It's not our horse," he said simply.

They were slightly taken aback by the unwelcome, but undeniable, truth of it.

"I think," said William at last, slowly, "that it's a sort of wild horse. I mean, there were wild horses all over England once, and they jus' belonged to anyone who could catch 'em."

"Yes, but that was in anshunt times," objected Henry. "There aren't any wild horses now. They've all died out or been caught."

"How do you know?" William challenged him.

"How do you know they have? There's forests an' things they could hide up in. I bet this is a wild horse that's been hidin' up in forests an' things, an' now it's come out an' we've caught it."

"It doesn't *seem* very wild," said Douglas.

"'Course it does," persisted William. "Look at it. All long hair an' suchlike."

"Yes, but it doesn't *act* wild."

"Well, I bet they don't all act wild. I bet there's some of 'em born sort of quiet. Same as schoolmasters. Most of 'em act wild, but some of 'em act quite quiet. It's jus' the way they're born. It's the same with wild horses."

"It's got horseshoes on," said Douglas.

"Well," began William slowly, obviously trying to reconcile this with a state of wildness, but Ginger interposed before he had found a satisfactory explanation.

"Seems to me more like it belonged to someone who's dead," said Ginger. "That's what I think, anyway. The man it belonged to's dead, an' it was tryin' to find someone else to belong to. It acted jus' like that, din't it? An'—well, look at it. It's not had its hair cut or its face washed or anythin' for ever so long. Stands to reason it mus' belong to someone who's dead. If he'd been alive he'd have looked after it—washed its face an' so on. Well, if the man it belonged to's dead, then it belongs to anyone that finds it. Stands to reason."

"I don't know if that's the lor," said Henry doubtfully.

"I bet it is," persisted Ginger. "Stands to reason it is."

"Well, anyway," said Douglas with the air of one who offers the complete solution of a mystery, "even if it doesn't belong to someone who's dead, it mus' be a stray horse. It was sort of wanderin' about the field as if it didn't know what to do. An' so we oughter take care of it till we find out who it belongs to."

"Yes," agreed William, "an' we've not time to start findin' out to-day, 'cause I've gotter go to that thing at the Vicarage this afternoon. Anyway, I've always wanted to have a horse, 'cause there's a thing in my penknife for takin' stones out of their shoes."

"We could ask people if they know whose it is," suggested Douglas tentatively. Douglas's conscience was always a little more tender than that of the other three.

"No, we couldn't," said William firmly. "We'd only get thieves comin' tryin' to steal it once people knew we'd got it. No, we'll jus' keep it till we've got time to start findin' out who it belongs to. We'll put it away in the ole barn now 'cause it's lunch time, an' we'll come back to it this afternoon. Gosh! I wish I hadn't got to go to that ole thing this afternoon. I'll come as soon as I can, anyway."

They led their unresisting steed into the barn, took off saddle and bridle, fetched a bucket of water, several armfulls of grass, and a whole pound of sugar, which Ginger had shamelessly filched from his mother's store-cupboard, and left it surveying its surroundings with an air of detached interest.

William allowed himself to be garnished and burnished for the afternoon with unusual meekness.

After all, there would be all the evening and all the next day to ride the horse. The next day he might do something really spectacular. If he could get hold of a banner he'd like to ride through the village streets with it, his Outlaws following behind. Or he'd like to put on his helmet and breastplate (he had an old saucepan and tray that filled these rôles) and charge Hubert Lane and

his gang, pursuing them over the countryside and finally
taking them prisoners. The only drawback was that any
such public and spectacular appearance might attract the
attention of the horse's missing owner, and William had
quite decided that it would be foolish to do that. All in
good time. No use rushing things. More haste less speed.
There were, in fact, quite a lot of copy-book maxims to
support his decision.

"I do hope, dear," Mrs. Brown was saying, "that
you'll sit very quietly through the speech."

"What's it going to be about?" said William.

"I really don't know, dear," said Mrs. Brown. "I
suppose I must have had a notice." She burrowed
among the papers on her writing-desk. "Oh, here it is!
The Upbringing of Children, by Mrs. Gladhill."

"Gosh!" said William. "Who's she?"

"I don't know, dear. I believe she's written books and
things. I expect she hasn't got any children. They
generally haven't." She sighed. "It's so much easier to
know how to bring them up, if you haven't got any."

But it turned out that Mrs. Gladhill had. Or rather she
had one—a dainty, docile, beautifully mannered little
girl of seven called Frances Mary. And Frances Mary
was at the Vicarage with her mother. It would have been
foolish indeed of her mother to leave her behind, for
Frances Mary was a living, breathing, moving testimony
to the success of the methods advocated by her mother.
She was, as it were, her stock in trade, for Mrs. Gladhill
made quite a good thing out of her lectures and books.
*The Mothers' Vade Mecum* was in its sixth edition, and
*Frances Mary and Her Mother*, published last month,
had been sold out before publication. Frances Mary
herself was quite a cult among childless elderly ladies,
and many a mother had copied the large butterfly bow

that adorned Frances Mary's golden curls. There were those who called her "smug" and "priggish," and even used such hard words as "impossible" and "intolerable," but perfection always has its detractors.

The two had arrived at the Vicarage for lunch, a meal at which Frances Mary had displayed, with much unction, the table manners for which she was justly famous, and at which Mrs. Gladhill had carefully pointed out to the rest of the company any of the more attractive traits of the child that might otherwise have escaped notice. Soon after lunch the members of the Women's Guild began to arrive. As the day was warm and sunny, the meeting was to be held on the lawn. Mrs. Gladhill went out to her audience accompanied by the Perfect Child. She introduced the Perfect Child to them, then said: "And now, Frances Mary, go back to the drawing-room and stay there quietly. Mrs. Monks will kindly let you look at her photograph albums." She flashed her brilliant smile at her audience. "I never let Frances Mary listen to my lectures. A child's brain should not be over-strained."

Frances Mary smiled sweetly at the gathering, then trotted off into the house. The accustomed murmur of admiration followed her. Mrs. Gladhill threw a benign glance around, cleared her throat, and began majestically: "Fellow mothers . . . "

She was well under weigh when Mrs. Brown and William arrived. There had been a slight hitch in their preparations, owing to William's having been discovered to be wearing odd shoes—both for the same foot—when they were half-way there. William protested passionately that it didn't matter, that he never kept his shoes for special feet, anyway, that he always wore any shoe on any foot, and both shoes and feet were used to it.

He said that no one would notice the fact that they were of different pattern unless they were balmy, and then it didn't matter what they thought. But Mrs. Brown was determined that for once in his life William should do her credit. So, by the time they had returned home, found the missing shoe, put it on, and made their way again to the Vicarage, Mrs. Gladhill was just beginning the exposition of her third rule for the upbringing of the Perfect Child.

There was an unusually large attendance of members, most of whom had come in a spirit of curiosity in order to see the much advertised Perfect Child at close quarters. It had even been rumoured that she would recite a poem of her own composition after tea.

Fortunately, however, there were two empty seats, one in the back row and the other in the middle. William hastily claimed the one in the back row, and Mrs. Brown, throwing him an anxious glance, but feeling assured that there was no possibility of his getting into mischief, hemmed in as he was on one side by the churchwarden's wife and on the other by the postmistress, made her way to the other seat. William sat for two minutes, giving his whole attention to the speech, before he came to the conclusion that it wasn't worth it. He looked round furtively and began to consider the possibilities of a large bush that grew just behind his chair. The possibilities were, he decided, more worthy of his attention than the speech. Slowly, and by degrees, he edged his chair back towards it. Whenever he did this his neighbours turned to look at him, but always when they did so he was sitting motionless, his eyes fixed earnestly on the speaker. At last he had edged it back so far as to be practically outside their range of vision. And then, quite suddenly, he vanished. When next his neighbours turned to look at him, he wasn't there. Without sound, without movement, as it seemed, he had disappeared— disappeared as completely as if the earth had swallowed him up. They were slightly puzzled, then dismissed the subject from their minds and gave their attention once more to the lecture. He wasn't their business, and the lecture was. They'd paid for their tickets and they meant to get their money's worth, boy or no boy.

William emerged from the shrubbery at the other side of the Vicarage and heaved a sigh of relief. He couldn't have gone on listening to that awful stuff a moment longer. It would be all right. He'd be back in his place by the time she'd finished, and his mother would never know he'd been away. He might even have time to slip over to the old barn and see how the horse was getting on. Ginger and Douglas and Henry would be having rides on it. It was jolly hard lines on him, not being able to be there, too. Well, it wouldn't do any harm to go and watch them just for a minute or two and then come back. He wouldn't stay long. Suddenly, he became aware of a little girl watching him from an open French window. She was a definitely attractive little girl, with golden hair, blue eyes, and rosy cheeks. She looked at him with interest and distinct favour. Though not of prepossessing appearance, William, fresh from his mother's hands, was radiantly neat and clean, his hair sleeked back, his collar shining, his tie in place, his stockings well gartered, his shoes decorously tied and a-gleam with polish. Definitely a nice little boy, such as her mother had no objection to her knowing.

"Hello," she said.

"Hello," he replied with an ingratiating smile.

"What's your name?"

"William. What's yours?"

"Frances Mary. . . . What are you doing here?"

"Me?" he said vaguely. "Oh, I'm jus' sort of walkin' round a bit."

"Have you come to the meeting?" she asked.

"Oh, yes . . . yes. I've been to the meeting. I've jus' come from it."

"Why've you come from it?" said the little girl. "It's not over, is it?"

"I'VE GOTTER GO AND HAVE A LOOK AT A HORSE OF MINE,"
SAID WILLIAM PROUDLY.

"No, it's not over," admitted William, "but I've gotter go an' have a look at a horse of mine."

The little girl stared at him, obviously impressed.

"Have you got a horse?" she said.

"Me?" said William. "Oh, yes, I've got a horse all right." He gave a short laugh implying that the idea of his not having a horse was ludicrous in the extreme. "Course I've gotter horse."

"Of your very own?" said the little girl, still in an awestruck voice.

"Course," said William, momentarily disallowing the claims of Ginger, Douglas and Henry to their joint property. "Like to come and have a look at it?"

"I'd love to," said the little girl, "but I don't think mother would like me to."

"Oh, yes, she would," persisted William, "I'm sure she would. Why shouldn't she? She likes you havin' a good time, doesn't she?"

"Oh, yes, but—I've got to go out there and have tea with them all as soon as she's finished speaking. I'm going to recite, too. Something I've made up myself."

She spoke with pride, but there was a certain undercurrent of humility. After all, even the reciting of a piece of one's own composition paled before the possession of a real live horse.

"Oh, well, I've gotter be back for tea, too," said William. "It won't take two minutes to go an' look at this horse of mine. It's only across a field. We'll be back long before it's time for tea."

The little girl obviously weakened.

"Well, I could just come and *look* at it, anyway," she said. "After all, it's natural history—isn't it?—and mother thinks that's very important."

"Oh, yes, it's that all right," said William.

"Yes, I'll come," said the little girl. "P'raps I'll be able to make up a poem about it afterwards."

"Oh, yes, I bet you will," said William. "It's a jolly good horse."

She came out of the French windows and walked sedately with William across the lawn to the gates. In the distance could be heard the clipped emphatic tones of the speaker.

"She can speak for a whole hour without stopping, except to take drinks of water," said the little girl proudly.

"This horse of mine," said William, "can run for hours and hours without drinks of water at all."

"She's been to America," went on the little girl.

"This horse of mine's been everywhere," said William.

They had reached the old barn now. The big horse was ambling good-naturedly across the field with Ginger on his back. Douglas and Henry walked proudly on either side, holding the bridle.

William stopped.

"That's my horse," he said casually.

Frances Mary was impressed.

"What a *lovely* one!" she said. "Isn't it big! Who are those boys?"

"Oh, they're jus' friends of mine," said William. "I said they could ride on my horse while I was away. I say"—he turned to her—"would you like a ride?"

Her eyes shone.

"Oo, I'd love it."

"All right," he said generously. "You have one. You have as many as you like. Hi, Ginger! Get off my horse."

They stared at him, so much impressed by his

immaculate appearance and the beauty and daintiness of his escort, that they did not even dispute his claim of sole ownership.

William introduced his new friend with an airy wave of his hand.

"She's called Frances Mary, an' she wants a ride."

Ginger scrambled down obediently, and they stood round Frances Mary, looking from her to the horse.

"How's she goin' to get up?" said Douglas.

"Oh, we'll push her up," said William. "Come on!"

Willing hands pushed the excited Frances Mary on to the saddle. She held on for one ecstatic moment, then, as soon as the horse took a step forward, fell off on the other side. The fall did not hurt her, as the ground was soft and muddy, but it altered her appearance to a considerable extent.

She got up laughing.

"Again! Again!" she cried. "Help me up again!"

Again willing hands pushed her up on to the saddle. Again, at the first step forward of the grey horse, she rolled off on the other side. Again she leapt up, muddy and laughing.

"Isn't it *fun*?" she said. "Do it again."

The Outlaws' admiration for her increased. They called her a sport. They hoisted her up again and again. Again and again she fell off. Her frock was torn and grimy, her hair ribbon came off, her hair fell about her face, her face was covered with mud. She was laughing and shouting in a way in which the Perfect Child had never laughed and shouted in her life before.

After the tenth fall, they hoisted her up yet again.

Now the horse was an amiable animal, but he was getting bored. These young creatures had been climbing on and off him nearly all day. He had followed them originally for sugar, not for donkey work. It occurred to him suddenly that he was fed-up, and that he'd like to go back to his field for a spot of peace and quietness. No sooner had he formed this decision than he acted on it, setting off at a determined canter, careless of the fact that Frances Mary had just been hoisted up on his back for the eleventh time. Frances Mary clawed the air wildly then lurched forward on to his neck, to which she clung with both arms. Shouts of delight came from her.

"I'm staying on, William. Look! I'm staying on."

The grey horse went at a quick trot towards the open gate that led into the next field. The Outlaws, alarmed, called to it to stop. It quickened its pace. Frances Mary still clung on, shrieking with delight. The horse kept determinedly in front of the Outlaws. When they ran to try to catch him up, he ran too. When they walked, he walked. And all the time Frances Mary clung on, shrieking with delight. All semblance to the Perfect Child had gone. She was transformed into a little savage with no thought for anything but the glorious exhilaration of the moment. The grey horse reached the road and cantered along it with its hilarious burden, the Outlaws running behind, imploring it to stop. Ginger even threw a piece of sugar at it, but it was beyond the seductions of sugar. It would be satisfied now with nothing short of home and liberty. The road back to its own field led past the Vicarage gates. It was just passing these gates when a large traction engine appeared, coming from the opposite direction. The grey horse did not like traction engines. It stopped, snorted, then galloped in at the Vicarage gates.

Mrs. Gladhill was drawing to the close of her lecture. She had described the method of bringing up children in much detail and emphasised its success in the case of her own child. "Several of you have remarked to me to-day," she said, "on the beautiful manners and behaviour of my own little girl. They are not some freak of nature, but merely the result of correct upbringing." She then invited questions. A woman in a purple hat in the second row got up and, with a side glance at Mrs. Brown, asked how one could counteract the contaminating influence of other children. She went on to say that certain children in the village had a most pernicious influence over other children. Again she glanced at Mrs. Brown. Mrs. Brown assumed an air of lofty detachment. At least, she assured herself, no one could have anything against William this afternoon, because she'd seen him herself, nicely settled in a chair in the back row, looking the picture of cleanliness and good behaviour. No, no one could have anything against William this afternoon, at any rate. Patiently, Mrs. Gladhill replied that it was all a question of the right method. Any child brought up on the right method would be an influence for good among other children. "I could trust my little girl," she ended with a bright smile, "among any children."

It was at this moment that the grey horse entered the garden and galloped clumsily across the lawn, upsetting several of the tables laid for tea. He was ridden by a crumpled, torn, dirty little girl who yelled and screamed with delight. "It's running! It's running! And I'm staying on!"

She had by now accustomed herself to the horse's motion, and was sitting more or less upright, and using the reins. But suddenly the horse recognised his own field across the hedge of the Vicarage. He leapt forward, shooting the little girl off his back, and, cantering through the side gate that someone had obligingly left open, disappeared from view.

"FRANCES MARY, WHAT *HAVE* YOU BEEN DOING?"

The little girl sat, still laughing, on the lawn, where he had thrown her, the centre of a horrified group. She was, indeed, hardly recognisable as the Perfect Child. But her mother knew her. Her mother gazed at her, growing paler and paler as she took in each detail of her dishevelment.

"Frances Mary," she faltered at last, "what *have* you been doing?"

THEY HARDLY RECOGNISED HER AS THE PERFECT CHILD.

Frances Mary laughed up at her through her mask of mud and tangled curls.

"I've been having a simply *lovely* time," she said.

Mrs. Brown glanced round fearfully for some trace of William.

The empty seat in the back row was all she could find.

# Chapter 3

# William Helps the Cause

William and his Outlaws sat in the old barn, plunged in thought. Once more the lady with the blue eyes and golden hair had visited the school to appeal for funds for her pet housing scheme. Once more the Outlaws, moved wholly by the blue eyes and golden hair, and with only the haziest notions of the object of her appeal, had decided to give all the assistance in their power. On the occasion of her last visit their help had taken an entirely practical form. Having vaguely grasped that the lady's efforts were aimed at ejecting large families from small houses and establishing them in larger houses, the Outlaws had taken all the children of a large family from the cottage in which they were staying, and had found accommodation for them at the Hall, in the absence of its owners and without the knowledge of the caretaker. Subsequent complications had proved—to the Outlaws' surprise and indignation—that the family did not wish to leave its cottage, nor did the owners of the Hall wish to accommodate the surplus population of the neighbourhood.

"This time," said William, "we'll jus' get money for it same as she said."

"How?" asked Douglas simply.

"She said do work for our parents an' get paid for it," Ginger reminded them.

"What sort of work?" said William, who had been so much engrossed by the blue eyes and golden hair that he hadn't listened to the lecture at all.

"Work in the garden an' that sort of thing," said Henry.

"Huh!" said William contemptuously. "Yes, I know. Weed all day for a penny an' then get the penny taken off you 'cause you pulled up a few flowers by mistake."

"Yes," agreed Ginger. "Chop up firewood all day for a penny an' get it taken off you 'cause you chopped up the wrong stuff by mistake."

"We've gotter think of some *big* way of makin' money," said William.

"What sort of big way?" asked Douglas.

"How can I know that when I've not thought of it yet?" said William irritably. "There mus' be big ways of making money. There wouldn't be any millionaires if there wasn't."

"There's kidnappin'," said Ginger. "People in America make a jolly lot of money doin' that, an' it's not much trouble."

"We've tried that," said William, "an' it didn't come off. The people we kidnapped never seemed to know they were kidnapped, an' no one seemed to want to pay money for 'em."

"Well, there's other things," said Douglas vaguely. "There's buyin' things an' sellin' 'em again."

"Yes, but you've gotter have some money to start buyin' 'em with," said William. "That's no good to us."

"Well, there's others. There's—there's inventin' somethin' no one's ever thought of before."

"I've tried that," said William bitterly. "I invented somethin' to clean chimneys 'stead of brushes, an' I only got covered with soot an' everyone got mad at me. They took money off me 'stead of givin' it me."

"Well, there's—there's lots of things."

"I've tried everything there is," said William. "I've hunted for hidden treasure for hours an' hours an' *hours* an' I've not found any. An' I've dug down all over our garden, tryin' to find a gold-mine. I got in an awful row last week diggin' down in the rose bed 'cause I found a stone what looked as if it had gold in it. I bet there's a gold mine there all the time if only people'd let me have a proper dig at it. They're always sayin' they want you to be useful an' they get mad the minute you start tryin' to be."

"I'd sell my motor boat if I could find anyone that wanted it," said Ginger.

"Well, you're not likely to," said William, "not since you took all the works out."

"Well, I put them back again," said Ginger, "all 'cept the ones I'd used to mend my watch with."

"They didn't make much difference to your watch."

"No, but I'm goin' to have another try sometime, an' arrange them differently. I think, p'raps, I put some of 'em in upside down. Anyway, it looks all right without 'em."

"Yes, till you put it in the water," said William. "Then it goes over on one side an' sinks. Oh, well, let's shut up about your motor boat. It's money we want, not motor boats. Anyway, it's jus' about tea-time an' I'm goin' home. There's bein' red jelly for tea, an' if I'm late they won't let me have any. We'll all come back here after tea. Someone may've got an idea by then. Kidnappin' would be all right if you could do it without kidnappin' anyone. It's the people you kidnap that always mess it up so."

They separated, and William walked homeward, his

mind busy with the problem of how to eliminate the element of the kidnapped from the process of kidnapping.

Robert was already at his place at table when William entered the dining-room.

"I SAY," SAID WILLIAM, "DO YOU KNOW ANY WAY OF MAKIN' MONEY QUICK?"

"I say, Robert, do you know any way of makin' a lot of money quick?" said William, as he sat down and, eyeing the jelly with anticipatory relish, reached out for a slice of bread and jam.

Robert did not answer. Robert had worries of his own. Or rather a worry. It was a worry that, he told himself, was unreasonable, ridiculous, morbid. But still it continued to worry him. It worried him in his dreams as well as in his waking hours.

It had happened two months ago when he went to a party at Victor Jameson's. A friend of Victor's whom he had not met before had been there—a tall, dark, sophisticated youth of about twenty-one called Edmond Montgomery. The three of them had been discussing money-lenders and the process known as "backing a bill". Victor and his friend confessed to a complete ignorance on the subject.

"What exactly is it?" Edmond Montgomery had said. "I mean"—he turned to Robert—"suppose I wanted to borrow, say, two hundred pounds, from a money-lender, and you were going to back the bill, what would you write?"

"Oh, that's quite simple," said Robert, anxious to show off a non-existent worldly knowledge. He took a small diary from his pocket, tore out a page, and wrote, "I, the undersigned, hereby guarantee to pay you two hundred pounds, should Edmond Montgomery fail to pay it in the course of the next two months."

Then he dated it, signed his name, and handed it to Edmond with a flourish.

"By Jove!" said Edmond inspecting it. Then he laughed, said "Thanks awfully," slipped it into his pocket, and began to talk of something else. And ever since then Robert had felt slightly uncomfortable.

Edmond Montgomery had not appeared in the neighbourhood after the day of the party, and it seemed that Victor knew him only very slightly. He lived somewhere in London, but no one, not even Victor, was quite sure where. The whole affair had begun to take on a sinister aspect in Robert's thoughts. Suppose that the words he had written were legally valid. . . . Suppose that the thing was a trap and that Edmond Montgomery had actually borrowed 200 on the strength of it without ever meaning to pay it back. . . . The thought made Robert break out in a cold perspiration at night. In the daytime it didn't seem so bad. In the daytime he was sure—or, rather, almost sure—that Edmond Montgomery had no intention of using the note, even if it were legal. In the night he was quite sure he had. And £200! What on earth had possessed him to make it a sum like that, a sum so vast that no one he knew had ever possessed it? It must have been the claret cup. He oughtn't to have had three glasses of the stuff. He wasn't used to it. . . . He hadn't liked to mention his fears to Victor, as he was sure that Victor would laugh at him. Indeed, he laughed at himself. He most determinedly laughed at himself. It was, he told himself, a most ridiculous idea to have got into his head. Still—he would be glad when to-day was over. To-day was the last day of the two months. He supposed that if Edmond Montgomery had borrowed the money and couldn't pay he'd hear from the money-lender to-day. He'd had an awful dream last night in which the money-lender (a dreadful man with a white face and black moustache and flames pouring out of his mouth) had dragged him off to an underground dungeon where he had to stay till he'd paid the £200. Again the sheer magnitude of the sum staggered him. Gosh! What a fool he'd been!

Wrapped, therefore, in his own gloomy thoughts, he merely answered "Shut up" when William spoke to him. Despite this, however, William's ideas were clarifying. A plan was forming slowly in his mind. He ate his tea as quickly as he could (contenting himself with only three helpings of jelly) and hastened back to his friends.

"I've gotter plan," he announced importantly. "It's a jolly good one, too."

"What is it?" said Ginger.

"Kidnappin'."

"Well, we've tried that an' it's no good. We said we wouldn't bother with it again."

"Yes, but my plan's a jolly clever one," said William. "We'll kidnap ourselves."

"We'll what?" said Ginger, taken aback.

"We'll kidnap ourselves."

"How can we?" said Henry somewhat indignantly. "How can anyone kidnap themselves?"

"*We* can," said William, "an' we're jolly well goin' to. We'll jus' go away an' hide somewhere an' write kidnappin' notes to our fathers till they send the money."

The Outlaws were silent for a moment. Then Douglas said slowly, "It's goin' to be jolly difficult."

William waved away the difficulty with an airy gesture.

"Oh, no," he said, "it's goin' to be jolly easy the way I've thought it out. You see—well, we'll jus' stay away in hidin' like I told you an' write notes to our fathers askin' for money an' then when they've sent it we'll come back an' they'll never know there wasn't a real kidnapper. Kidnappers get a jolly lot of money, too. They get as much as a hundred pounds a person."

There was another silence—this time eloquent of doubt.

"I bet my father wouldn't pay a hundred pounds for me," said Ginger. "You should hear the way he goes on about my school bills and suchlike."

"Why do they want to send us to school, then?" said William passionately. "That's what I'm always sayin'. Grumblin' about school costin' so much an' still makin' us go there! Seems batty to me. Whenever my father starts grumblin' about how much money I'm costin' him, I always say I don't mind stoppin' goin' to school, but he never takes any notice. What I think is——"

"Let's get on with this kidnappin' plan," interrupted Douglas, knowing that William, once mounted on his favourite hobby horse, was difficult to dislodge.

"All right," said William, dismounting reluctantly. "But I think this school business is—oh, all right. Well, now for this kidnappin' plan. We'll just go away in hidin' same as I said."

"I bet they'll know it's us," said Henry.

"Know what's us?"

"Know it's us doin' it. I mean they'll think it's funny that jus' us four have got kidnapped an' no one else. They're always so suspicious."

"Y-yes," William allowed this point. "Yes, they are. Seems 'straordinary to me that no one ever seems to trust us. We trust them all right, but they never seem to trust us back. Always nosin' about tryin' to find out what we're doin' an' to stop us doin' it. Why, only last week——"

"Well, about this kidnappin' plan," said Douglas again firmly. "We'd better get it fixed up if we're goin' to do it at all."

"Course we're goin' to do it at all," said William

indignantly. "What d'you think I've thought it all out for if we're not goin' to do it? Well, if we're not all goin' to be kidnapped, how many of us shall be?"

"Three," said Ginger.

"Two," said Douglas.

"One," said Henry and backed up his suggestion by adding: "If it's three or two of us, they'll start gettin' suspicious an' thinkin' we've fixed it up, but if it's only one, they can't."

"Yes," said William thoughtfully, "yes, there's something in that. Yes, I bet we'll do that. Well, I'll be the one."

The others did not dispute this. They were accustomed to William's taking the leading rôle in any drama they enacted.

"An' we'll write the letter together," he went on briskly. "I bet we'll write a jolly good letter."

"When shall we start?" said Ginger.

"We'd better start now," said William, "'cause it's Saturday afternoon an' my father's at home. We'll want some paper and a pencil."

Douglas ran home to fetch them, and when he returned the other three had concocted the letter. Ginger wrote it out in large uneven capital letters.

DERE SIR I HAVE KIDNAPED YOUR SON WILLIAM AND WILL PUT HIM TO DEATH WITH HORRYBLE TORCHURE UNLES YOU SEND A HUNDRED POUNDS IMEDATLY. PLESE BRING THE MONY TO THE OLD BARN AND LEVE IT JUST INSID THE DOOR. YOURS TRUELY KIDNAPER.

They put it in an envelope and addressed it to Mr. Brown.

"Of course," said William, "none of *us* must take it to
him. It'd start him gettin' suspicious at once if we did
that. We'll have to get someone else to take it to
him. . . . Tell you what. I've got an idea. Go down to
the road an' see if you can see anyone comin' along an'
send him the letter with a message. I've got a jolly fine
idea for a message. You'll have to do it alone 'cause I've
gotter go into hiding."

He gave them their instructions and they went down
to the stile that led from the field into the road and sat
there waiting. The road was empty at first, but within a
few minutes the form of a small boy appeared proceeding along it in the distance. He proceeded in the erratic
fashion peculiar to small boys, disappearing every now
and then into the ditch, kicking a stone from one side of
the road to the other with a good deal of elaborate foot
play, walking along the parapet of a small bridge that
spanned the local stream, climbing on to the top bar of a
gate, and jumping down from it, aiming an imaginary
pistol at a cow who was peacefully asleep in a field. . . .
As this form came nearer it turned out to be that of
Johnny Smith, one of the junior inhabitants of the
village.

Ginger hailed him.

"Hi! Johnny Smith!"

Johnny Smith slipped his imaginary pistol into his
pocket and approached them cautiously.

"Uh-huh!" he said, a sound intended to be both
greeting and query. Ginger handed him the letter in an
impressive manner.

"Will you take that to Mr. Brown?" he said. "William's father, you know."

The small boy regarded the note with obvious
suspicion.

"Why can't William take it himself?" he said.

Ginger assumed an expression of exaggerated innocence.

"We don't know where William is," he said. "We've not seen him for quite a long time."

"GIMME THE PENNY FIRST, AND THEN I'LL TAKE THE NOTE."

"Why can't you take it, then?" said Johnny Smith.

"Me?" said Ginger. "Oh, I'm not goin' that way."

"Neither am I," said Johnny Smith promptly.

Ginger sighed. He had hoped, from motives of poverty rather than uprightness, to be able to conduct the affair without resort to bribery.

"We'll give you a penny if you'll take it," he said.

"All right," said Johnny Smith. "Give me the penny first an' then I'll take it."

"We've not got it yet," said Ginger. "We shan't have it till to-night. We promise we'll give it you to-morrow. Word of honour."

"All right," said Johnny Smith, knowing that among the few virtues the Outlaws possessed was that of keeping their promises. "Gimme it."

"No, you've gotter listen to this," said Ginger, still retaining the grubby missive. "You've gotter say that a boy gave it you to give to him an' that the boy said it was given to him by a man in a black mask. An awful man, say. Very big with awful-looking eyes."

"I thought you said he'd gotter mask on," said Johnny Smith.

"Yes, he had," said Ginger. "I mean, he looked as if his eyes'd look awful if he hadn't gotter mask on. Say that he looked as if he could easy put anyone to death by torchure if they didn't do what he wanted. Say he'd got jus' that sort of look."

"All right," said Johnny Smith unconcernedly. "Gimme the letter. An' I'll come for the penny to-morrow."

"Yes," said Ginger. "Don't forget to tell him about the awful man in the black mask."

"All right," said Johnny Smith and, taking the letter, continued his erratic progress down the road.

Ginger, Douglas, and Henry returned to the old barn and reported to William that everything had, so far, gone according to programme. They then took up a position behind the hedge, from which, unseen, they could watch Mr. Brown placing the £100 inside the barn door.

"We won't give all of it to that house thing, will we?" said Ginger. "We'll keep a bit for ourselves."

"A hundred pounds!" breathed Douglas. "Gosh! We'll be able to buy a jolly lot of things with that. All the things we've ever wanted."

"We'll give some to that house thing," stipulated Henry. " 'Cause that started it."

"He ought to have got the letter now," said William rather nervously, and added: "Of course, he may not bring *quite* a hundred."

"Well, ninety would be all right," said Ginger.

"Or eighty," said Douglas.

"Or seventy," said Henry.

They waited for some minutes in a tense silence. No agitated parental figure appeared running to the old barn with bank-notes in its hand.

"P'raps he had to go to the bank for the money," suggested William. "He may not have quite a hundred pounds. I dunno how much money he's got. He's always grumbling that he hasn't any money, but he always seems to be able to buy things."

"Fifty would be all right," said Ginger.

"Yes, fifty would be all right," agreed the others.

Again they waited in silence. They could not know, of course, that Johnny Smith's erratic course had taken him to a spot where the brook was so wide that it had to be crossed on stepping-stones. It was a point of honour with Johnny Smith to cross these backwards, and, in doing so, he had overbalanced and only just saved himself from falling into the water. In recovering his balance he let go the letter which slipped down between the stones and began to float slowly away on the current. With great presence of mind, Johnny Smith hastened to the bank, seized as long a stick as he could find, and began to try to bring the letter to land with it. He secured it and pulled it along the bed of the stream to the bank. It escaped several times, but each time was secured once more, and finally was brought to land. Johnny Smith picked it out and examined it carefully. It was sodden. There was a large hole in the middle where the stick had gone home. There were several other holes. It was covered with mud. It was not such a note as can be delivered by one gentleman to another with any credit to either. Johnny Smith, having come to this conclusion, crumpled it into a sodden little ball and threw it back into the stream. He felt no qualms of conscience. He was to have been paid a penny for delivering the letter. He would not deliver the letter nor would he claim the penny. Nothing, in Johnny Smith's eyes, could be more honourable, and straightforward. Any complications that might ensue from the non-delivery of the letter did not concern him. In any case, they would probably not occur to-day, and to-day was all that mattered to Johnny Smith. To-morrow was far enough away to take care of itself. So Johnny Smith, brandishing his stick and once more kicking a stone along the road with a still more finished exhibition of foot play, passes out of the story.

The Outlaws sat in a silence that became steadily gloomier and gloomier as the minutes went by.

"Doesn't look as if he thought much of you," said Ginger at last.

"I bet he thinks as much of me as yours does of you,"

retorted William with spirit. "P'raps he's gone out to try'n' sell somethin'. He's jus' got a new mowing machine. P'raps he's tryin' to sell that."

"He won't get a hundred pounds for a mowing machine," said Henry.

"He might for this one," said William. "It's a jolly good one. It's got handles an' it's much greener than the old one an' makes more noise."

"P'raps we ought to have said in the letter that we'd take less than a hundred pounds," said Henry.

"Forty would be all right," said Douglas.

"Or thirty," said Ginger.

"Or twenty," said William. "Well," coming down suddenly to hard facts, "we wouldn't mind half a crown."

"Or even sixpence," said Ginger wistfully.

"Tell you what," said William. "Go down an' have a look round an' see what he's doin'. He may've had a fit or fainted with fright or somethin' when he got the letter."

Ginger and Douglas made their way cautiously down to the Browns' house, while William and Henry remained in hiding, still expecting each moment to see the agitated form of Mr. Brown appearing on the horizon. But the only forms that appeared were those of Ginger and Douglas returning from their scouting expedition.

"He's jus' sittin' in the mornin' room readin' a novel," announced Ginger.

"*Well!*" said William indignantly. "Fancy him sittin' in the mornin' room readin' a novel while I'm bein' put to death by horrible torchure."

"No, you're not," said Henry, the literal.

"I am for all he knows," retorted William. "I'm

havin' my legs an' arms an' everythin' pulled off for all he knows while he's sittin' in the mornin' room readin' a novel!"

"Let's write another letter," suggested Ginger. "One that'll really frighten him."

"P'raps he's afraid of comin' up here," said Douglas. "P'raps he's afraid we'll kidnap him, too. Shouldn't be surprised if that's it, that he's afraid to come here."

"All right," said William. "Let's fix a different place."

"They gen'rally do it in churchyards," said Henry with his rather irritating air of omniscience.

"All right," said William, "let's do it in a churchyard. Well, come on. Let's start on another letter."

The second letter was the result of much thought, of earnest—even acrimonious—discussion. Mr. Brown had remained unmoved in the face of danger threatening his son. He would not surely remain unmoved in the face of danger threatening himself. The note was short and vague, but none the less ominous. It dispensed with ceremonial address and began: "To Mr. Brown," continuing: "Unless the money is handed over before eight o'clock to-night, it will be the worse for you. Bring it to the hole in the wall in the churchyard. Kidnaper."

Henry, whose mind was not quite happy about the spelling of the last note, had fetched his dictionary and had looked up every word except the last, about which no one felt any doubts. They put it in an envelope, addressed it to Mr. Brown, and gave it into the charge of the first small boy they met with the promise of a halfpenny (they considered that they had overpaid Johnny Smith) the next day, if it should be safely delivered. The small boy was conscientious, but a newcomer to the neighbourhood. He found his way to the

Browns' house just as Robert was setting out from the front door.

"Is your name Brown?" said the small boy.

"Yes," said Robert apprehensively.

"Well, this is for you," said the boy, thrusting the letter into his hands.

Robert tore it open with trembling fingers. Then the colour faded from his face, and his heart began to beat violently. It had come! His worst fears were justified. The money had to be paid to-night. Kidnaper. That must be the name of the money-lender. It sounded foreign. It was printed in a large illiterate hand, but, of course, money-lenders were illiterate. He'd seen one in a play once done by the Hadley Amateur Dramatic Society—a greasy old man in a dressing-gown, counting over his money in a squalid little room by the light of a flickering candle stuck in the mouth of a bottle. He was a miser. All money-lenders were misers, of course. He glanced at the letter again. Eight o'clock. Gosh, it was nearly that now.

There wasn't even time to consult a lawyer. In any case lawyers were almost as bad as money-lenders. He'd seen a film about a lawyer once, and in the end the lawyer had pinched every penny of the hero's money and the hero ended up in the workhouse or somewhere. Better keep clear of lawyers. He looked round wildly. Should he confess everything to his father? No, he couldn't bring this terrible disgrace upon his father's head. His father wasn't a bad chap as fathers went. A bit of a stick-in-the-mud, but so were most fathers. In any case he'd gone out and wouldn't be back till after ten. His mother? No, it would kill his mother. He must face the thing alone. They must not know till he'd done all he possibly could to stave off the disgrace. Probably he couldn't stave it off for long. He might be taken to prison this very night—or, at the latest, to-morrow morning.

Gosh! What a fool he'd been! Two hundred pounds! It would teach him a lesson that he'd never forget all the rest of his life. There probably wouldn't be much of his life left. He didn't know how long he'd have to spend in prison. Two hundred pounds! Gosh! He glanced at the clock again. It was five to eight. Good heavens, what was he to do? He came to a sudden decision. He'd take what money he had, and go and throw himself on the man's mercy. He'd promise to bring him all his money till he'd paid off the debt. He'd never be able to marry Felicia Mendleson now, but he wasn't so sure that he wanted to. She'd let him down very badly in the Doubles Final at the Tennis Tournament. She'd gone all to pieces and served double fault after double fault. He wouldn't have minded so much if she'd been suitably apologetic, but she'd behaved as if he were to blame. She'd have made a rotten wife. . . . His mind returned to the £200, and again his heart sank. How on earth was he ever to get £200? He'd never even known anyone with so much money. Well, the first thing to do was to go and meet this Kidnaper man in the churchyard, and throw himself on his mercy. He'd better do it now, too. It was close on eight. The meeting-place suggested in the letter did not strike him as in any way peculiar. The money-lender in the film had transacted all his business through a kind of grid in a tumble-down hovel, and none of his clients was ever allowed to see him face to face. Probably this Mr. Kidnaper was one of the same kind. . . .

The Outlaws crouched disconsolately in the field next to the churchyard wall, at the point where one of the stones had fallen out, leaving a gap. (They had used this spot before in their games, and had more than once been chased out of the churchyard by an indignant sexton.)

Dusk had now fallen and they were feeling cold and disgruntled.

"It'd've been better if we'd tried one of our fathers," said Ginger. "Yours doesn't seem much good. I'm jus' about sick of hangin' round wastin' my time like this when I might have been doin' somethin' useful."

"You shut up," said William indignantly. "He may be comin' any minute. He's only jus' about got the note. It's a jolly good plan an' you'll be jolly glad I

WILLIAM GAVE A GASP AS HE RECOGNISED ROBERT.

thought of it when we've got the money."

"Yes," echoed Ginger bitterly, "when we've got the——"

He stopped suddenly. Someone was coming through the churchyard in the dusk. They crouched down silently, holding their breaths. Yes, he was coming towards the hole in the wall. He had come right up to it.

"I'VE BROUGHT ALL THE MONEY I'VE GOT. I PROMISE TO BRING THE REST AS SOON AS I CAN."

He had stopped. William gave a gasp as he recognised the figure. It was Robert. Robert! What on earth was Robert doing here?

Robert bent down to the hole.

"Hello," he said in a hoarse unsteady voice.

"Yes," whispered William cautiously.

"I've brought all the money I've got," panted Robert. "It's only one pound, four and fivepence half-penny, but I promise to bring the rest as soon as I can. I mean, I shall be leaving college next year and getting a job, and I'm sure to have a salary of some sort, and I'll pay you half every year—more than half, if it's anything like a decent one—till I've paid it all. And I've brought my watch and my camera and the new horn I'd just got for my motor cycle. They're all quite good ones. Here they are!"

He pushed a pound note, eight sixpences, four pennies and three halfpennies, the watch, camera, and motor horn through the hole.

"I say," he went on, "it'll be all right, won't it? I'll let you have the rest as soon as I've got it."

There was a silence. William was too deeply moved to speak. That it should be Robert who was doing this for him, Robert, who usually seemed unaware of his existence or who only recognised it in order to act the tyrant; that Robert should come here, hoarse with emotion, to pay the ransom for him, while his father read novels by the morning-room fire. . . . Robert must be fonder of him than he thought. Robert must, in fact, be deeply attached to him. He'd try to be nicer to Robert in future. He'd—but the long silence had broken Robert's nerve. He had turned away abruptly and was running as fast as he could through the dusk to the gate and out into the road.

"One pound, four and fivepence halfpenny," Ginger was saying. "Well, it's not bad considerin' I was beginnin' to think we weren't goin' to get anythin' at all."

"*An*' a watch," said Douglas.

"*An*' a camera, *an*' a motor horn," said Henry, surveying the spoils with satisfaction.

"We're not goin' to keep 'em," said William firmly. "It was jolly nice of him to bring them, but we're not goin' to keep 'em—'cept"—the memory of the blue eyes and golden hair returned faintly, dimmed by the passage of several hours—"about two an' six for that house thing."

"Why?" said Ginger.

"'Cause we're jolly well not," said William firmly, "an' that's why."

"That's no reason," objected Ginger.

"Yes, it is," said William pugnaciously.

Reluctantly they assented. As a matter of fact each knew that he would have felt the same in William's place.

"All right," said Ginger, "give him back the pound an' the other things, but keep the five and fourpence."

"No," said William firmly, "we're only keepin' two and sixpence for that house thing, an' we'll give the rest back to Robert. Jolly kind of him tryin' to buy me back like that, 'stead of sittin' readin' a novel while I'm bein' torchured to death same as my father did. I've a jolly good mind to buy him somethin' for his nex' birthday. I didn't think he thought as much of me as that. Fancy payin' one pound four an' fivepence halfpenny for me! As well as all the other things! I s'pose I am jolly useful to him. I've posted letters for him sometimes an' that sort of thing, an' once I cleaned his motor cycle for him when he wasn't there, though he was mad when he came back an' found I'd done it, 'cause it wouldn't start, but I bet that wasn't my fault, anyway.''

"Well, let's go home now," said Ginger. "It's bed-time an' I'm sick of hangin' about here like this. It's been a rotten game, an' I votes we don't play it again.''

"It's not been a game," said William severely. "We've been workin' hard gettin' money for this house thing same as she said we ought to. An' we've got two and sixpence an' I bet that's jolly good.''

"I thought we were goin' to get a hundred pounds," muttered Douglas.

"Yes, an' we might have done," said William bitterly, "if my father hadn't of rather sat readin' novels than save me from bein' torchured to death. I'll remember that next time he talks about all he's done for me an' suchlike.''

"Oh, well, let's get on home," said Henry, yawning. "I don't think there's much in this kidnappin' business. It's about the third time we've tried it, an' it never comes to anythin'. I think I'll stick to bein' a chimney-sweep when I'm grown-up, after all. I don't think kidnappers have much of a time. I'm jolly sorry for them.''

Robert was sitting alone in the morning-room staring moodily in front of him, when William arrived. Perhaps he ought to leave college and get some sort of a job at once, even if it were only working on the road. It was ghastly, to have this terrible debt of—he paused while he wrestled with mental calculations—one hundred and ninety-eight pounds, fifteen shillings and sixpence half-penny hanging round one's neck. He didn't even know whether the man would allow for the watch and camera and motor horn. He wished he hadn't taken them now. He ought to have stayed and got a receipt, too. Gosh! What a hole he was in!

"The man's let me go, Robert," said William.

Robert turned sharply and glared at him.

"Who's let you go?" he snapped. "What do you mean? Don't talk nonsense. Go away."

Didn't want to be thanked, thought William appreciatively. Lots of noble people were like that, of course. He hadn't realised till to-day how noble Robert was. But he must thank him, and tell him about the money and things. He must make up a convincing story about the kidnapping, too. He didn't want Robert to find out that there hadn't really been any kidnapping after being so noble about it.

"He didn't really hurt me at all, didn't this man," went on William. "He jus' kept me chained up in a sort of underground dungeon. I couldn't tell you where it was," he added hastily, "'cause he blindfolded me when he took me there. I say, it was jolly decent of you, Robert."

Robert glared at him still more fiercely.

"Are you mad," he said, "or are you trying to be funny? Because if you're trying to be funny——"

"You mus' just let me thank you, Robert," broke in William feelingly. "I know you don't want to an' all that sort of thing, but, anyway, the man din't really want all that money. He asked for it, I know, but—but"—William searched for a moment for some reasonable explanation of this sudden change of attitude on the part of the kidnapper. Then it came in a sudden flash—"he heard this afternoon that his aunt had died an' left him some money, so he didn't want any more 'cept two and sixpence. He jus' wanted two and sixpence to pay his train fare to where he lives. He sent the rest back. Here it is." William laid on the table the pound note, three sixpences, four pennies and three halfpennies. "An' there's your things. He didn't want them either."

He pointed to the chair by the door, and Robert saw his watch, camera, and motor cycle horn, which William had put there as he entered the room. Robert's bewildered gaze went from the money to the chair by the door and from the chair by the door to William.

"What on *earth*——" he began, but at that point the door opened and Victor Jameson entered. He held a book in his hand.

"Hello, Robert," he said breezily. "Here's that book you lent me. Sorry I haven't brought it back before. I quite forgot it." He opened it, and took a paper out. "I've just found this in it. Do you remember it? It's that document you made out for Edmond Montgomery, backing a bill for two hundred pounds. He was reading this book that night, and he must have slipped it in as a book-mark." He threw the paper carelessly on the table. "Like to come for a walk, old chap?"

Robert snatched up the paper and examined it. Then he turned to the little pile of money that William had left on the table and began to count it. Two and sixpence missing. Two and sixpence. . . . That wretched boy had babbled something about two and sixpence. *He* was at the bottom of this. He was at the bottom of everything. He turned on him savagely to demand an explanation.

But William had vanished.

Something in Robert's face had told him that a full and accurate account of the kidnapping business was going to be extracted from him, and he had hastened to give the two and sixpence into Ginger's charge while there was yet time.

# Chapter 4

# William and the Bugle

William had not joined his School Historical Society because he was fond of history, but because he had heard that the members would be allowed to miss afternoon school on the day of their termly expedition. He realised, of course, that the expedition might be even more boring than afternoon school, but at any rate it would be a change. William liked changes. No one could ever accuse him of getting into a rut.

The history master did not receive his application for membership with enthusiasm.

He knew William only slightly, but what little he knew had not inspired him with any desire to extend the acquaintance. He was a quiet well-conducted man, passionately interested in history, and he liked quiet well-conducted boys passionately interested in history. He knew that William was neither quiet nor well-conducted nor passionately interested in history.

Still, William had applied for admission to the Society, and he felt that he had no adequate grounds for refusing him, though he decided grimly to stand no nonsense and to eject him on the first excuse.

The Autumn Term expedition was to be made to an Elizabethan manor house whose grounds contained several Roman remains. William heard this unmoved. He was not interested in Elizabethan manor houses, nor

was he interested in Roman remains. He was much
relieved, however, by the discovery that he would miss
an arithmetic lesson by taking part in the expedition.
The arithmetic master shared something of his relief.

But when the day came he was feeling far from
cheerful. A friend of Robert's had been over the afternoon before. Like all Robert's friends he had been
distant and unbending in his manner to William, and it
was quite by accident that William discovered he was a
kind of super scout (his official designation was a Rover)
and that he possessed a bugle. He had even brought a
bugle with him, though he did not perform on it. He had
brought it with him in order to give it into Robert's
keeping for two days while his own family was removing.

"Things get lost, you know," he explained, "and I
shouldn't like anything to happen to it. It's rather a good
little bugle."

This had happened the day before the day of the
expedition, and on the afternoon of the expedition
Robert had gone out, leaving the bugle in the top drawer
of his dressing-table among his collars and handkerchiefs.
William knew that it was there, because he had watched
through the keyhole to see where Robert put it. He dared
not have entered the room, of course, while Robert was in
the house, but this afternoon—the afternoon of the
expedition—Robert had gone to tea and supper with a
friend who lived in the next village but one. William had
been longing to try his hand at the bugle ever since he
heard of its existence, and it seemed the irony of fate that
it should be left unguarded the very afternoon that he
would be away on the Historical Society's expedition.

William, however, was not the boy to sit down meekly
and accept the irony of fate. After all, he might be glad
of something to relieve the monotony of the Historical

Society's expedition, and what more suitable to relieve the monotony of anything than a bugle? Robert would be out of the house before he started for the expedition and would not return till after he was in bed. Robert would leave the bugle safely in his drawer among his collars and handkerchiefs, and find it safely there on his return. No harm would be done to anyone. William did not even intend to use the bugle as a means of annoying the history master. He intended to be very careful indeed, especially as the history master had never yet been known to return any confiscated article to its owner. He did not intend to blow one note upon the instrument. He merely intended to flourish it, to swagger with it, to raise it to his lips for imaginary blasts, to pose before his friends and enemies as the Boy who Possessed a Bugle. He felt that it would be a secret consolation for whatever rigours of boredom the expedition might have in store for him.

The history master—whose name was Mr. Perkins, and who was known familiarly as Ole Warbeck—eyed him with disfavour when he found him waiting with the other members of the Historical Society at the appointed meeting-place. Though he wished the boy no real ill, he had hoped that he would have been prevented—by, say, a slight cold—from coming on the expedition.

William met his gaze with a look of bland innocence, holding the bugle well concealed beneath his coat. The charabanc arrived, and the members scrambled on to it. Mr. Perkins sat on the front seat next to Blinks Major, the Secretary of the Society, a thin earnest boy with spectacles, who knew all the dates in English history, and had asked his father for a book on Roman Britain for his last birthday present. William sat on the back seat and drew his bugle from its hiding-place.

A LOUD AND INHARMONIOUS BLAST RENT THE AIR.

Mr. Perkins, discussing hypocausts with Blinks Major, turned round, frowning, at the sound of hilarious mirth from the back of the charabanc. William sat gazing dreamily in front of him, surrounded by giggling neighbours. Mr. Perkins glared at him suspiciously, then turned round, and resumed his discussion with Blinks Major.

"There's an excellent example of the hypocaust at Northleigh Villa," he said, "but——" Again the sound of uproarious mirth made him frown and turn round

"GIVE THAT TO ME, BROWN," MR. PERKINS SAID STERNLY.

quickly. Not quite quickly enough, however. Again William was gazing dreamily in front of him, apparently unaware of the uproar around. He returned to Blinks Major and the discussion upon hypocausts. Again the uproar broke out. Again he wheeled round—just too late.

He could not know, of course, that as soon as his back was turned William raised the bugle to his lips, and with exaggeratedly puffed out cheeks blew imaginary blasts upon it. It does not take much to amuse small boys in holiday mood, and William was flattered and raised a trifle above himself by the appreciation accorded to his performance. Trying to outdo all his previous efforts, he drew in his breath and—inadvertently let it out with his lips upon the instrument. A loud and inharmonious blast rent the air. Mr. Perkins wheeled round. William had been too much surprised to move. Mr. Perkins's face went as red as William's.

"Give that to me, Brown," he said sternly.

William handed the offending instrument up to the

front seat. Mr. Perkins put it with some difficulty into his overcoat pocket.

"And you needn't ask me for it back," he went on, grimly, "because you won't get it."

"He'll have to give it me back," said William apprehensively to his neighbour. "It doesn't belong to me."

"Well, he won't," his neighbour assured him with relish. "He's never given anythin' back that he's taken away. He wouldn't even give Timpkins his watch back that his godmother had given him the day before. His father went an' made an awful fuss, but he wouldn't."

William, of course, knew that this was true. His mind went fearfully to Robert. Robert would return to-night and find the bugle that had been entrusted into his keeping vanished. There would ensue a scene—or rather a series of scenes—of which William hardly dared to think. Robert, his father, his mother, Robert's friend, seemed to tower above him like outraged giants thirsting for vengeance—Robert, most of all, for Robert would feel that his friend's trust in him had been betrayed, and his wounded honour would seek outlet in exacting the utmost penalty from William. A faint hope that the blame of the vanished bugle could be laid upon burglars was dismissed as soon as it arose. No one would have the slightest doubt as to who had taken the bugle from Robert's drawer. His schoolfellows, in any case, would be sure to spread the news. William looked wistfully at the mouth of the bugle that protruded from Mr. Perkins's pocket. It would probably be easy enough to extract it in the course of the day, but that would not solve the problem. Mr. Perkins would have no doubt as to who had removed it and would take immediate steps to secure its return. No, there seemed no solution of the problem that he could see. . . .

He dismounted gloomily from the charabanc and inspected with grim disfavour the grey stone walls of the ancient castle.

"Huh!" he said scornfully. "Fancy comin' all this way to see that ole thing."

"Come along, boys," called Mr. Perkins fussily from the front, pushing William's bugle farther down into his pocket. "Don't dawdle there."

They straggled into the entrance hall, where the guide awaited them.

William listened without interest to an account of the various dates at which the various parts of the castle were built. The party straggled into the banqueting hall. A stream of dates and historical names again flowed unheeded past his ears while, in imagination, he faced an infuriated Robert. His eyes again wandered wistfully to the bugle that protruded from Mr. Perkins's pocket. He wished he'd never touched the beastly thing. It was going to be the worst row he'd ever got into in all his life. The party followed the guide out of the banqueting hall towards the staircase. William straggled along at the end. At the foot of the staircase a small passage ran off at right angles and turned a corner. It looked rather an interesting little passage, and William felt a sudden desire to know what was round the corner. The other members of the Historical Society were surging ahead. No one was looking round. He slipped along the passage and turned the corner. Another little passage with a closed door at the end. . . . Having satisfied his curiosity about the passage, William now felt an irresistible longing to satisfy his curiosity about the door. He approached it and listened. No sound came from within. The room—if room it was—must be empty. He'd just open it, peep in, then run back to join the Historical

Society on their journey up the stone staircase. He opened it and peeped in. A small sunny sitting-room, furnished in a refreshingly modern manner, as it seemed to William, who had just come from the banqueting hall. . . . At first he did not see the old lady who sat in a bath-chair by the window, wearing a shawl. He did not see her, in fact, till she said sharply:

"Well, come in, come in. . . . Don't stand there like that."

William was so taken aback that he obeyed automatically.

"And you should knock at the door before you open it," went on the old lady severely.

William gaped at her, still too much taken aback to speak. The old lady glanced at the clock.

"And you're ten minutes late," she continued. "You were late yesterday, too. You must——" She looked at him and broke off. "A different boy again," she commented. "Dear, dear! I never knew anyone like you modern boys. Aren't you ever satisfied with a job? Why did the other boy go?"

"I don't know," said William truthfully.

"Well, come along. Don't waste any more time. Push me out into the garden. I'm tired of telling a different gardener's boy every day what to do. I don't know whether it's the gardener's fault or yours that he can't keep a boy." She looked William up and down. "In your case it'll be yours, I expect. You don't look as if you could keep any job for more than a day. Well, hurry up. You've wasted half the morning already."

William hesitated. She seemed rather annoyed, and he felt that any explanation of the true state of the case would only annoy her still further. And, after all, wheeling the old lady round the garden would probably be as interesting as following the guide round the rotten old castle, with everyone jeering at him for having had his bugle confiscated.

"Push me out into the garden," went on the old lady, "and wheel me gently round the path. *Gently*, I said. What on earth does the boy think I am? Don't jerk the chair about like that. Smoothly and *gently*. . . . "

It was a small, private-looking garden, enclosed by a yew hedge. William wheeled her round the path.

"What's your name?" said the old lady suddenly.

"William."

"That's better than some of them. The last was called Percival. His friends called him Perce. You're called Bill, I suppose?"

William gave a non-committal grunt.

"You're smaller than the others," went on the old lady. "You must be small for your age. Are you glad to have left school?"

William gave a gasp of envy. So the boy he was supposed to be had left school. Lucky beggar! Then slowly he became the boy who had left school and his face radiated triumphant freedom.

"Yes, I jolly well am," he said.

"Why?" said the old lady.

William began to expound his views on the general uselessness of education, the waste of time involved, the wear and tear of brain power, the continual interference with other and more useful pursuits.

"I can't think why someone hasn't stopped it years ago," he ended eloquently. "They stop slavery an' cruelty to animals an' suchlike an' yet they let a thing like school go on an' on an' on."

The old lady chuckled.

"Yes," she said, "I quite see your point of view. I used to feel just like that about it myself when I was your age. However, we've both left now so we can crow over people who haven't. By the way, there's a party of them coming round to-day. Generally my nephew doesn't let anyone come round while I'm staying with him, because I dislike people poking and prying about the place when I'm in it, but this boys' school wanted to come over, so he let them. Unlike you and me, he has a great respect for educational institutions. I wonder if they've arrived yet. Did you see them?"

"Yes," said William.

"Nasty little things. I hate boys. What did they look like?"

"The boys looked all right," said William. "I didn't like the look of the master, though."

"No, you wouldn't," said the old lady, "and I don't suppose he liked the look of you."

They had reached a garden seat and she raised her hand imperiously. "Stop here. You may sit down on the seat. I've never been so badly wheeled before in my life. I'm almost bumped to death."

William sat down on the seat and stared in front of him, still lost in gloomy contemplation of the scenes that would take place when the loss of the bugle was discovered, thinking with ever increasing bitterness of Mr. Perkins, who was even now wandering about the historic mansion with his ill-gotten booty sticking out of his coat pocket.

"Well, don't go to sleep," said the old lady sharply. "Tell me something more about yourself. What do you do when you aren't working? When you aren't supposed to be working, that is. I don't suppose you ever really work. What sort of games do you like playing?"

"WHAT DO YOU DO WHEN YOU AREN'T WORKING?" ASKED
THE OLD LADY.

William tore himself from visions of vengeance to
come, and began to describe the more exciting adventures that had recently befallen him—flights from irate
landowners, pitched battles with rival gangs, Red Indian
treks through the woods, then, throwing accuracy to the
winds, went on to tell of his more imaginary exploits as a
spy, as a Scotland Yard detective, as a Commander-in-
Chief of the British Army.

The old lady chuckled again.

"I wish I'd known you sooner," she said. "I mean I

wish I'd known you when I was a child. I think we'd have got on very well together. I used to have adventures just like that. I remember once I climbed to the top of the Great Pyramid and held thousands of Arabs at bay for three days till the rescuers arrived. Another time I boarded a pirate ship, alone and unarmed, locked them in the hold, and took the ship into the nearest harbour and handed the pirates over to justice. There were about a hundred of them."

"I once did that, too," said William, much interested.

"What are you going to be when you are grown up?"

"Well, I've not quite made up my mind whether to be a detective—a high-up detective, I mean—or a chimney-sweep."

"I couldn't make up my mind whether to be a pirate or keep a sweet shop."

"Yes, both those are jolly good," agreed William. "I've thought of them, too."

At that moment they caught sight of a large figure in an opulent fur coat being shown into the little sitting-room.

"Good Lord!' moaned the old lady. "It's Mrs. Polkington. I can't face her. She stays for hours and talks about the 'Cause'."

"What Cause?" said William.

"The Cause of the moment. It's always a different one, but she always says just the same things about it. She's one of those women who have the energy of ten ordinary women—and no wonder, because they drain everyone they come across bone dry. She leaves me feeling like a piece of chewed string. I don't know why I'm telling you all this. I wouldn't have told any of the other boys. But I feel that we have a lot in common, and I tell you frankly that the thought of being talked to by that woman for the next two hours . . . "

"I'll stop her coming out to you," volunteered William.

"You can't. No one can."

"Let me try anyway."

"No, you couldn't possibly."

"I bet I could."

"You'd be rude to her or tell her lies, and I won't have that."

"No, I bet I can stop her without doin' either."

"Well, if you can, I'll give you anything you like. In reason, that is."

"All right," said William and set out towards the sitting-room.

The lady in the fur coat had dismissed the housemaid with a wave of her hand ("I see where she is, my good girl. Don't trouble to announce me") and was just stepping into the garden by the French window when she found William barring her way.

"She doesn't want to see you," he said.

His voice was low and respectful. He gazed at her sadly.

She stopped and stared at him.

"What do you mean?" she said haughtily.

He glanced at the figure of the old lady in the garden and lowered his voice confidentially.

"Well," he said, "I don't know if I ought to tell you."

"Do you mean that she's ill?" said Mrs. Polkington. "If she's ill I must certainly go to her. She'll need me."

"Well," said William again in a mysterious voice, "I—well, I wouldn't go to her if I was you, that's all."

"But why not?" said Mrs. Polkington, impressed, despite herself, by William's manner.

"She's—well, no one knows about it yet."

"Knows about *what*?"

"Of course it *may* not be that."

"May not be *what*?"

William sighed.

"Perhaps I oughtn't to have told you."

"You haven't told me anything," snapped the visitor.

William assumed a look of deep perplexity.

"I oughtn't to tell you," he said, "but—well, it isn't fair to let you go near her. Not till they know for certain. Of course if it isn't smallpox——" He clapped his hand to his mouth as if he had inadvertently let out a secret. "There now, I oughtn't to have told you."

"Smallpox!" said the lady, her eyes starting out of her head. "Good gracious! I always say that it's about a lot still, but people keep it dark. Smallpox! Fancy!"

"They don't know it's smallpox yet," said William hastily.

"What does the doctor say?"

"He's not been yet."

"I saw him at Gorse Villa as I came along. I suppose he's coming over here next. I thought he looked a bit worried. No wonder! Why on earth did that girl let me come into the house at all?"

"She doesn't know about it," said William.

"I suppose that's as well. You won't have a servant left in the house when they do. You're the gardener's boy, aren't you?"

"Uh-huh," said William.

"A new one again?"

"Uh-huh."

"There's a new gardener's boy every time I come here. I hope you'll work hard and try to keep the job. You'll be the first that has done, if you do. Well, I shouldn't go too near her if I were you. She's very wise to stay in the open air like that. Nothing like open air for carrying germs off. I'm a great believer in it myself. Give her my love and sympathy, won't you?"

"Yes," said William.

"Good-bye and remember—don't go too near her."

She went hastily out of the room and out by the side door, staying to shake from her coat any germs that might happen to be clinging there.

William returned slowly to the old lady.

"You don't mean to say she's gone?" said the old lady.

"Oh, yes, she's gone all right," William assured her.

"How did you do it?"

"Oh, I jus' did it," said William nonchalantly.

"Were you rude to her?"

"No."

"Did you tell her any lies?"

"No," said William, "I didn't say anything that wasn't true."

"Well, you're the only person who's ever managed to get rid of Lucy Polkington. Did she send a message?"

"Yes. She sent you her love an' sympathy."

"Sympathy. Why sympathy?"

"She jus' said that. She jus' said love an' sympathy."

"Well, she's gone—which is the main thing. I felt I couldn't have endured her to-day. There are certain people whom one can't endure on certain days. I'm very grateful to you, William. Let me see, I promised you anything you wanted, in reason, didn't I? What would you like?"

"A bugle," said William.

"A *what*?"

"A bugle."

"Why a bugle? I don't know anything about bugles. Don't you want anything but a bugle?"

"No, I'm afraid I don't," said William. "It doesn't matter if you've not got one, but it's the only thing I want jus' now."

"*Why* do you want a bugle?"

"Well, I can't quite explain," said William slowly. "It's sort of rather a long story. But it's jus' the only thing I want jus' now."

"You'll get the sack if you start on a bugle. One of them—it was either Perce or Syd, I've forgotten which— got it for a penny whistle. What about a nice pencil-case?"

"No, thank you," said William politely.

"Or a nice penknife?"

"No, thank you," said William, still more politely.

The old lady sighed.

"Well, I've never seen anyone worst Lucy Polkington before in all my life, so let it be a bugle. But what *sort* of a bugle? I don't know anything about bugles. I expect there are hundreds of different kinds."

William was silent for some moments, then said:

"I saw jus' the sort I want to-day."

"Where?"

"That master that came with those boys had one sticking out of his coat pocket an' it was just the sort I want."

"How odd of him! What was he doing with a bugle sticking out of his pocket?"

"Well, he had one," said William, as if quite unable to explain the mystery, "'cause I saw it."

"Perhaps he uses it to call them together or something. Schoolmasters are always rather odd."

"Yes, p'raps he uses it for that," agreed William.

"Look! they're coming here. What a nuisance!
They've no right to come here. Oh, I remember, my
nephew mentioned that he'd given them permission to
come and look at the yew hedge. This wretched man
who's brought them is keen on gardening, it seems.
Here they are!"

"I think I'd better go an'—an' do a little weeding,"
said William, hastily diving out of sight behind a laurel
bush. His voice came muffled by distance and the laurel
bush. "Yes, there's a jolly lot of weeds here. I'll be some
time in here gettin' them up."

After a moment or two Mr. Perkins and his flock
entered the garden.

"Now listen, boys, and stop scuffling," said Mr.
Perkins in his thin, high-pitched voice. "This is one of
the most famous yew hedges in the country. Notice
the——" He caught sight of the old lady and took off his
hat with a flourish. "I beg your pardon, madam. I didn't
notice that the garden was occupied. Perhaps——" He
made a courteous gesture, as if to withdraw himself and
his flock.

"Oh, no," she said, "it's quite all right. My nephew
told me that he'd given you permission to show your
boys this garden. Look round by all means. I don't like
boys, but I realise that they're a necessary evil, which
reminds me . . . " She glanced at Mr. Perkins's pocket
from which the mouth of the bugle boldly protruded. "Is
that a bugle?"

Mr. Perkins followed her gaze.

"Er—yes," he said, slightly embarrassed. "Yes, it is
a—er—a bugle."

"May I look at it?" said the old lady.

Mr. Perkins took it from his pocket with a flourish and
handed it to her. She examined it curiously.

"And where can one buy such a thing?" she said.

"I—er—I'm afraid I really don't know," said Mr. Perkins, still more embarrassed.

"That's rather unfortunate," said the old lady, "I thought that as you carried one about with you you'd probably know something about them."

"Well—er—I dare say I could find out," said Mr. Perkins unhappily. "As a matter of fact——"

"Oh, never mind," interrupted the old lady. "Only I wanted to give one to a boy who'd done me a good turn." She glanced round for William. "The gardener's boy. He seems to be still weeding. He's a strange boy, but I promised him a bugle, and I haven't the faintest idea of how to set about getting one. When I found that you carried one about with you I thought that you might know."

"Well—er—" stammered Mr. Perkins, then suddenly an idea occurred to him. He beamed ecstatically. He had been afraid that there'd be trouble about this bugle. It probably didn't really belong to that little wretch, and its owner would probably raise hell to get it back. The boy's father might even take a hand and come interfering and trying to bully him, as young Timpkins's father had done. Well, he'd stood his ground over that, and he'd stand his ground over this, whoever came interfering and trying to bully him. He'd never given back a confiscated article yet, and he wasn't going to start now. But the process of standing his ground was always rather wearing. Irate letters from irate fathers, irate visits from irate mothers, demanding back what they considered was their property. How much simpler it would be if he could just say that he'd given the thing away! No one could insist on its return then. It would take all the wind out of their sails. And it would be a very graceful act to give it to this dear old lady, who wanted it for some deserving boy—the sort of boy, apparently, who did people good turns and weeded gardens and that sort of thing—a very different type from that little wretch Brown. He glanced round. Unfortunately that little wretch Brown didn't seem to be here. Dawdling about, he supposed, making a nuisance of himself somewhere or other, holding up the whole party when the time came for setting off home. He'd have liked him to be here to see his bugle given away. And he'd have liked the other boy to be here, too, so that that little wretch Brown could see a well-behaved boy—the very opposite of himself—being rewarded for his good behaviour. It might have been a useful object lesson.

He took the bugle from his pocket and handed it to the old lady with a courtly bow.

"I'd be most grateful, madam, if you would kindly accept this."

"Oh, but surely you need it, don't you?" said the old lady, taken aback.

"No, I don't," said Mr. Perkins firmly. "I—er—I never really use it, and I'd be only too grateful to you if you would accept it."

"Well," said the old lady, taking it into her hand, "it's a cumbersome sort of thing to carry about with you if you never use it. It'll ruin the fit of your coat. You're *quite* sure you don't want it? It's exceedingly kind of you."

"Not at all," said Mr. Perkins with another courtly bow.

"I'm sure the boy will be most grateful. He seemed set on a bugle."

"Please give it to him with my best wishes," said Mr. Perkins, "and tell him from me that I'm glad that it

"I'D BE MOST GRATEFUL, MADAM, IF YOU'D KINDLY ACCEPT
THIS."

should be given to someone who really deserves it."

After further exchanges of courtesies Mr. Perkins
conducted his flock out of the garden, and William
emerged from the laurel bush.

"Finished your weeding?" said the old lady.

"Yes, thanks," said William.

"What have you done with the weeds?" said the old
lady, looking round. "Eaten them?"

"Yes," said William absently, then hastily correcting himself. "No."

"Well, here's your bugle. I suppose you heard what happened?"

"Er—yes. I did sort of hear," admitted William.

"Yes, I noticed you were weeding pretty quietly. Well, you're in luck. It looks quite a good article of its kind. What on earth was the man doing carrying it round with him if he doesn't use it? Still, it was kind of him to give it to me. Saved me a lot of trouble and expense. I can't think why I made a rash promise like that. After all, I don't suppose you've kept Lucy Polkington off for long. She'll be round again before evening. Listen. . . . That's the charabanc come to take those boys away. Would you like to go and watch them set off? You can thank the man for giving you the bugle, too, if you like."

William made his way back to the front of the house where the boys were surrounding the charabanc. He held the bugle carefully hidden under his coat.

"Come along, Brown," snapped Mr. Perkins. "Late as usual! What have you been doing all this time? We're just on the point of starting. Come along, come along, come along. And"—he continued on a note of triumph and self-satisfaction—"it's no use your asking me for that bugle back, because I've given it away. Given it away, you understand? Given it away."

Still smiling a smile of self-satisfaction and triumph (*that* would teach the little wretch), Mr. Perkins climbed into the coach. William, too, climbed into the coach, still holding the bugle under his coat. The coach started off with its cargo of bored and weary boys. A short distance down the road they met a little crown of people, headed by Mrs. Polkington. It was the entire neighbourhood coming to see how the old lady's smallpox was. They had called at the doctor's and found him out. They all carried germicide in various forms in order to protect themselves from infection.

"We won't go into the house," they were saying. "We'll just ask at the door. Of course they may have taken her to an isolation hospital by now."

Mr. Perkins, pleased by the quietness and decorum of the exhausted boys, turned and threw a quiet glance round the charabanc. Then the smile froze on his face. That Brown boy sat, quite quiet and well behaved—so quiet and well behaved that one could have no possible handle against him—holding a bugle on his lap. A *bugle*. *Another* bugle. How on earth had he got hold of another bugle. Or—*was* it another bugle? Mr. Perkins's imagination fairly boggled. How could he have got hold of another bugle during the afternoon? And yet—how could it be the same? He'd given the original one to the old lady for her gardener's boy. This Brown boy couldn't, surely, have taken it from the gardener's boy. He was capable of anything. But, no, that was impossible. There wouldn't have been time. They'd set off almost as soon as he'd given it to the old lady. It was all most mysterious. *Most* mysterious. He fixed a stern gaze on William's face. William met the stern gaze so blandly and unflinchingly that Mr. Perkins turned round to ruminate over the problem in silence. His mind went round and round in a circle. How could it be the same bugle? And yet, how could he have got hold of another? And yet, how could it be the same? His mind began to feel dizzy. He wondered whether to accost William and question him, but decided not to. There was something in that bland and unflinching stare that warned him not to. He was the sort of boy with whom it wasn't safe to interfere unless you were absolutely sure of your ground, and Mr. Perkins wasn't absolutely sure of his ground. How could anyone be sure of his ground in the extraordinary circumstances?

"I thought the corbels in the banqueting hall were most interesting, didn't you, Mr. Perkins?" said Blinks Major conversationally.

"Most interesting," agreed Mr. Perkins absently, "yes—er—most interesting."

His mind was going round and round and round. How could it be the same bugle? And yet, how could it be another? And yet, how could it be the same? And yet, how could it be another? And yet, how could it be the same? He began to feel dizzier and dizzier.

\*        \*        \*

"Smallpox?" the old lady was saying indignantly. "Who on *earth* said I'd got smallpox?"

"The boy," replied Mrs. Polkington. "The boy who came to me in your sitting-room."

"Oh, the gardener's boy."

"I suppose so."

"Did he say I'd got smallpox?"

"Well, actually," said Mrs. Polkington, "he said that they didn't know whether it was smallpox yet, but naturally I——"

The old lady chuckled.

"I see." She looked round. "I gave him permission to go and see those schoolboys set off, and he's not come back yet. I expect he's got the sack by now, anyway. I told him he wouldn't keep the job a day. No, dear Lucy. I've not got smallpox. The boy, probably, misunderstood something I said. These boys *are* so stupid, you know. Oh, here's the gardener."

A rubicund, burly-looking man approached and touched his cap.

"I'm sorry the boy never turned up, your ladyship," he said.

"The new boy? Oh, he turned up all right, but I've not seen him for the last half-hour."

"Beg pardon, my lady, but he never come at all. I had a note from his mother to say that he'd broke his leg."

"But a boy *was* here."

"Beg pardon, my lady, no boy's been here to-day."

"But there was a boy here. I gave him a bugle."

"One of them schoolboys went off a-carryin' of a bugle," said the gardener. "An untidy-looking little varmint, he was."

"With his stockings coming down?"

"Yes."

"And his tie crooked?"

"Yes. I heard 'em call him William."

"William," said the old lady musingly. William. . . . Smallpox. . . . Bugle. . . . A most mysterious affair. But, probably, quite simple if one knew the explanation. Mysterious things always were.

She chuckled again suddenly.

"Oh, well, we've all had a little excitement this afternoon. William, probably, most of all."

# Chapter 5

# William and the Policeman's Helmet

It was with mixed feelings that William heard he was included in the invitation to the Christmas Eve party at Marleigh Manor. Sir Gerald and Lady Markham always gave a party on Christmas Eve, but, so far, only Robert and Ethel had been invited. This year William was invited, too. His spirits rose when first he heard of it, for a party was, after all, a party—an affair involving in its very nature such delicacies as trifles, jellies, iced cakes, and lemonade, delicacies that seldom came one's way in ordinary life. Then he remembered that Robert and Ethel would be present, and his spirits sank. For Robert and Ethel, whatever private differences they might have, united always, as it seemed to William, in a joint effort to prevent him from deriving any enjoyment from life. They'd completely spoil the party for him, of course. They'd shut him up the minute he opened his mouth to speak. They'd glare at him the minute he started trying to get a decent meal. Seemed to think a person's mouth wasn't meant to eat with or talk with. He wondered bitterly what they thought a person's mouth *was* meant for. . . .

Robert and Ethel, on their side, were little better pleased than was William himself.

"Can't think why they're beginning to ask kids," said Robert indignantly. "It won't be much fun with a lot of kids about." He turned to William. "You try making a nuisance of yourself and——" He looked at him darkly and left the threat unfinished.

"Oh, all right," said William. "You seem to think that I want you there any more'n you want me there. Grown-ups spoil any sort of party. They dunno how to *act* at them."

But Robert maintained a dignified aloofness and refused to be drawn into argument.

William became, however, deeply interested when he heard that Ronald Markham, a youth of about Robert's age, possessed a real policeman's helmet, which he had appropriated during a Cambridge "rag". William's eyes opened wide when he heard of it. A policeman's helmet. A real policeman's real helmet. It had always been one of his ambitions to try on a real policeman's real helmet. Perhaps Ronald would let him try it on. *Surely* Ronald would let him try it on. He might even lend it to him for an indefinite period, so that he could swagger about in it before an admiring crowd of friends and enemies. . . . William saw himself doing this, and drew a deep sigh of rapture. It was a wonderful vision, and there wasn't any reason why it shouldn't come true. There wasn't really any reason why Ronald shouldn't lend it him. It was the sort of thing that people often did in stories. Perhaps he, William, would save his life, and he'd ask him what he'd like in return, and he'd ask for the loan of the policeman's helmet, and then he'd *give* it him. In stories, people were always saving other people's lives and being asked to choose anything they liked in return. He'd had rotten luck so far in saving people's lives. He'd never had a decent chance. It was pretty rotten to think that he'd lived eleven years and never had a single chance of saving anyone's life, and being asked what he'd like in return. Never once in all those years had he seen anyone on the point of being run over by a horse (in which case he'd have leapt at the bridle and pulled it back) or mauled to death by a lion (in which case he'd have forced the lion back with a red-hot poker), or dying of poison (in which case he'd have given him a glass of antidote to drink). Still, it might happen any day, so he mustn't give up hope. And, even if he didn't save his life, Ronald would probably lend him the helmet. So certain was he of this that he felt quite cheerful when the day of the party arrived. A policeman's helmet. A real policeman's real helmet. . . . He did not confide his hopes in Robert or Ethel. He had learnt by experience that the less one said to Robert and Ethel the better.

Robert and Ethel, on their side, regarded him as one might regard a live bomb that might explode at any minute.

"If he starts any of his monkey tricks . . . " muttered Robert.

"I can't think why they *asked* him," moaned Ethel. "It's been such fun before. It'll be completely spoilt if they're going to start asking kids to it."

But they had not started asking kids to it, as it turned out. William had been asked solely as a companion to a young nephew of the Markhams, who was spending Christmas with them. He was of William's age, but not after William's heart. Walter Markham was an earnest intellectual boy, whose chief interest lay in his collection of wild flowers, and who shuddered with horror when William mentioned the white rats that he had bought with a recent tip. They had a brief conversation, in the course of which William elicited the fact that Walter was not interested in Red Indians or pirates or wild animals or smugglers, that he didn't like "rough games", and that his ambition in life was to become a schoolmaster, because it would give him so many opportunities of doing good. He had a passion for facts, and told William that his favourite reading was the encyclopaedia. After that, conversation languished, and William began to look around for other sources of entertainment. He soon discovered that these were limited, for the other guests, young people of Robert's and Ethel's age, had obviously no desire for his company. He had been asked there because of Walter, their attitude implied, and he must content himself with Walter. So he sat with Walter, morosely silent, till he heard the words "policeman's helmet" from the group near him. He pricked up his ears eagerly. . . . Yes, they were going to see the policeman's helmet. They were surging in a crowd upstairs to Ronald Markham's "study" (a room, by the way, in which he did almost everything but study) where it was kept. William followed, leaving Walter turning over the pages of an *Encyclopaedia Britannica* that he had found in the bookcase near. He hurried joyfully at their heels. At last he was going to see it, to try it on, even (for his optimism was a hardy organ) to have it lent him for a day or two. There seemed no immediate prospect of his saving Ronald Markham's life, so he was making up his mind to not having it actually given him. He followed them to the study door, caught a glorious glimpse of Ronald Markham putting on the helmet amid screams of laughter, and was on the point of entering when—the door was slammed in his face.

"We don't want kids here," said someone (Robert, probably), and "Who asked *you* to come up? Go down to Walter," said someone else (Ethel, probably).

William went slowly downstairs. Walter raised his head from his encyclopaedia.

"This is frightfully interesting," he said. "Listen. 'Adder's tongue: fern so called from shape of its fruiting spike.' I didn't know that, did you?"

William scorned to answer. He sat for some moments plunged in deep dejection, then his optimism came once more to his rescue. He knew that they were going to act charades after supper. He'd probably get a chance of wearing the helmet then. Yes, there wasn't any reason at all why he shouldn't take the part of a policeman in the charades and wear the helmet. Probably they'd ask him to. Probably they'd feel sorry they'd been so rotten about it upstairs, and would want to make up to him for it. Yes, they'd certainly feel like that. They'd want to make up for being so rotten to him. They'd choose a charade with a policeman in it, so that he could be the policeman and wear the helmet. William had an incurable faith in human nature, which no amount of experience ever succeeded in destroying.

Upheld by this confidence, he did full justice to an excellent supper, and, ignoring the frowns of Robert and Ethel, continued to eat for quite five minutes after everyone else had finished.

Supper had been served in the library, as the dining-room (the largest room in the house) had been cleared for dancing and charades. The charades were to take place first. As the choosing of sides went on, William hung about in the foreground, coughing significantly in order to draw attention to himself. No one, however, took any notice of him. It was rather rotten of them to leave him to the last, he thought aggrievedly, after the way they'd treated him over the helmet. Still—he reassured himself—someone would *have* to choose him sooner or later.

But no one did. When all the grown-ups were picked, Ronald turned casually to William and Walter, and said, with the air of one granting a great favour: "And you kids can watch if you'll keep quiet and behave yourselves."

"Good!" said Walter. "I can go on with the encyclopaedia."

"B-b-but I don't mind actin'," said William desperately. "I *like* actin'."

"We don't want kids," said Robert firmly.

"But——" began William.

"Shut up," said Robert and Ethel simultaneously.

William shut up, trying to put into his expression something of the indignation that he felt. It was wasted labour, however, as no one was looking at him. It was a nice way to treat him, he thought bitterly. He wished he hadn't come at all. It would have served them right if he hadn't come at all. He'd only come because of the policeman's helmet, and he'd hardly even seen it, so far. Wasn't likely to now, either . . . not as far as *they* were concerned, anyway.

The side that was to form the audience was arranging the chairs in rows with much laughter. William scowled at them morosely. Only thought about enjoying themselves. Never thought of other people. Hadn't even let him *look* at the policeman's helmet. . . .

They were leaving clear for a stage the space at the end of the room where there stood the large side-board on which was displayed the collection of Georgian silver of which Lady and Sir Gerald Markham were justly proud. Lady Markham looked at it fondly as she took her seat in the front row of the audience. Walter had fetched his encyclopaedia and was reading it with deep interest.

"Did you know, William," he said, "that 'airfoil' is 'surface suitably shaped so that when it is moved through air it experiences the maximum of reaction with minimum of wasteful resistance to motion'?"

William grunted absently. His thoughts were still busy with the policeman's helmet. After all, there wasn't any reason why he shouldn't just look at it. He knew where it was. If they wouldn't let him act they could hardly expect him just to *sit* for hours and hours and hours. . . . And he wouldn't do it any harm. He'd only just look at it and perhaps just try it on. He wouldn't do it any harm, anyway.

"I say," said Walter, "do you know what 'alchemy' is?"

There was no answer. He glanced up. William was not there. He glanced down again. He didn't really care whether William was there or not. He was a very uninteresting boy. . . .

William had made his way cautiously up the staircase. The coast seemed to be quite clear. The "acting side" of the charade party was assembled in the little room, known as the breakfast-room, at the farther end of the hall, discussing their charade. Shrieks of laughter came from them. . . .

William found his way to Ronald's study, opened the door, and entered on tiptoe. There was the policeman's helmet lying on the table in the middle of the room. William put it on, stood on a chair and looked at himself in the mirror over the mantelpiece. The effect—or so it seemed to William—was magnificent, stupendous. He got down from the chair and swaggered about the room, seeing himself as a tall, majestic, ferocious-looking policeman of enormous girth and height. From this imaginary eminence he scowled threateningly down upon imaginary criminals, clapped handcuffs upon them, hustled them off to prison. . . .

"*Would* you?" he said grimly through his teeth, as he tackled a gang of desperate dare-devils and by neat twists of ju-jitsu laid them all sprawling and helpless at

"*WOULD* YOU?" SAID WILLIAM GRIMLY, AS HE TACKLED AN IMAGINARY GANG OF DARE-DEVILS.

his feet. But the room began to seem too small a stage for his activities. Pursuing fugitives from justice, he found himself impeded at every turn by walls and doors and tables and chairs and fenders. . . . Running a particularly dangerous criminal to earth, he collided with a bookcase and rolled ignominiously upon the floor. He picked himself up, adjusted his helmet, which had slipped down over his eyes, and looked around him with disgust. How could anyone be a policeman properly in a place like this? He went to the window. . . . The garden stretched out, spacious and mysterious, in the darkness—a perfect place in which to track criminals and engage in hand-to-hand combats without knocking tables and bookcases over. He opened the door cautiously. The coast was still clear. The "acting side" was still discussing the "word" with much hilarity in the breakfast-room. Slipping the policeman's helmet under his coat (which but imperfectly concealed it), he crept down the stairs and out by the side door into the garden. There, he put on his helmet and started at once in pursuit of a gang of famous international crooks who had been hiding behind the yew hedge. He pursued them several times round the lawn, cornered them finally beneath the cedar tree, shot the ringleader, handcuffed the others, and drove them in front of him at the pistol's point into prison, which was the garage. In the course of this he had several times to adjust his helmet, which had a way of slipping down on to his nose, but this did not, in his own eyes at any rate, detract at all from his dignity. Having secured the crooks, he received the plaudits and congratulations of his superior officers with a modest smirk, and set off at once on the track of a desperate murderer, who had the blood of half the police force on his hands. He tracked him several times round the garden, through a shrubbery (on his hands and knees), and finally confronted him in the summer-house. A fierce struggle ensued, during which William was nearly worsted, but finally he tied up the murderer with some rope that he happened to be carrying in his pocket, and dragged him off to prison. Tiring of crooks and murderers, he stood in the middle of the lawn, a majestic, awe-inspiring figure, and directed innumerable streams of traffic, stopping cars or waving them on with imperious gestures, severely reproving erring motorists and dragging one or two of them off to join the crooks and murderers in the garage.

Suddenly he heard the opening of a door at the back of the house, the kitchen, probably. Suppose someone came out into the garden, saw him there, and haled him ignominiously indoors. . . . He "froze" for some moments behind a laurel bush, then made his way cautiously into the road. If anyone was looking for him in the garden, he'd stay in the road till they'd finished. He simply couldn't relinquish his policeman's helmet just yet. It would rob life of all its savour. A motor car stood in the road in the shadow of a tree. It stood in complete darkness—none of its lights turned on. It looked as if it had been there for ever—the sort of car that belongs to no one in particular and never has belonged to anyone in particular. He decided to hide in it for a few minutes till the coast should be quite clear again.

He climbed into the back seat and crouched, listening. There were no further sounds. He decided to stay there for a few minutes longer, however, in order to be on the safe side. He still wore his policeman's helmet, but the little interruption had brought him to earth. He was no longer a policeman. He was a boy playing at being a policeman. He hadn't captured all those thieves and brigands. He hadn't done anything. Nothing had happened. He heaved a deep sigh. Nothing ever *did* happen in real life. . . .

But he was wrong.

Something *was* happening in real life, and happening not very far away.

In the breakfast-room where the "acting side" had been planning the "word" with such hilarity, a horror-stricken silence reigned, and the man who had suddenly appeared between the curtain that hid the French window, with a revolver in his hand, addressed them curtly:

"Put your hands up," he snapped; "and I shoot the first one that moves or makes a sound."

They gaped at him like a set of panic-stricken rabbits, and put their hands up obediently, if shakily. He was a horrible-looking man, with unshaven cheeks, yellow eyes, and a crooked mouth.

In the dining-room the audience was growing slightly restive.

"What a long time they're being!" said Lady Markham. "Ah! here they come."

A man entered, carrying a sack. Not a feature of his face could be seen. A cap was pulled down over his eyes and a black handkerchief was tied round his face, just above his nose. A burst of clapping greeted his entrance.

"It's Robert!" cried Ethel.

"I think it's Ronald," said Lady Markham.

"Bravo!" cried the Vicar, clapping heartily.

The man proceeded to take the pieces of Georgian silver from the sideboard and put them into his sack.

"Gently, dear," murmured Lady Markham apprehensively.

"The word must be burglar or thief," said someone brightly.

"I'm *sure* it's Robert," said Ethel.

"I really think it's Ronald," said Lady Markham. "He's always so careful about details when he dresses

A MAN CARRYING A SACK ENTERED. NOT A FEATURE OF HIS
FACE COULD BE SEEN.

up. Look, he's even got a dreadful old pair of socks and shoes for the part. I know he's been getting things ready for these charades for quite a long time."

The man continued to put pieces of silver into his sack.

"IT'S ROBERT!" EXCLAIMED ETHEL.
"BRAVO!" CRIED THE VICAR.

"Bravissimo!" said the Vicar, clapping still more heartily.

"Be careful, dear," murmured Lady Markham. "I shouldn't like any of them to get scratched."

"I'm *certain* it's Robert," said Ethel.

The man put the last piece in the sack and went out of the room.

His exit was greeted with a renewed burst of clapping, and an excited discussion as to the word arose.

"I'm sure it's not burglar. That's too obvious. It must be something more subtle."

"Of course, there are hundreds of words that mean stealing. Kleptomania or some word like that. . . . We'll just have to keep an open mind and see what the other scenes are. . . ."

"Anyway, whoever it was, it was *splendid*, wasn't it?"

Meantime, the man in the breakfast-room was addressing the still panic-stricken "acting side".

"Now, I'm going to stand behind this curtain for five minutes," he said, "but I'll still be pointing my gun at you, and if anyone moves or makes a sound he'll be plugged."

He withdrew behind the curtains, put the pistol on a small table with the barrel pointing through the curtains, then lightly, without a sound, went out of the French window and across the garden to the road. The "acting side" still continued to stare in fascinated horror at the barrel of the pistol. . . .

*        *        *

No, William was thinking, nothing ever happens in real life . . . when a sack of bricks, as it seemed to him, was flung down violently upon him, two men leapt into the front seat of the car, and it started off down the road with a jerk. William was silent, simply because the impact of the heavy sack had completely winded him. When his breath returned he was still silent. He had had time to think while his breath was returning, and his thoughts were not reassuring. He was evidently trespassing in someone's car, and he strongly suspected that his presence would not be welcome to the owners.

The best thing would be, he decided, to lie low till the situation had clarified a little. He might, of course, manage to escape from the car as secretly as he had entered it; but, just at present, there seemed no chance of escape. The car was travelling quickly along narrow lanes, with very uneven surfaces. An unusually violent bump sent a large silver teapot out of the sack on to his nose. He removed it cautiously and regarded it with interest. So the sack wasn't full of bricks or logs as he'd thought. It was full of teapots. Odd. . . . What were they doing carrying sacks of teapots about? Another bump brought a cream jug into his eye. William regarded it with still deeper interest. Perhaps they were going to have a picnic. A picnic in the woods in the middle of the night. Odder still, but rather intriguing. His spirits rose as he considered the prospect, and heartening visions came to him of joining in the picnic, of finding that the two men were quite jolly after all (anyone planning a picnic in the middle of the night must be jolly) and consuming large quantities of sausage rolls, cakes, and fruit or whatever they'd brought. After all, it was getting on for an hour since he'd had supper and he was jolly hungry again. He felt the sack with his hands in order to discover what provisions the picnickers had brought. . . . It all seemed to be crockery—jugs and teapots and things. There didn't seem to be any food at all. And an enormous amount of crockery and stuff for a picnic for just two men. William couldn't understand it. . . . What would they want with all those silver teapots and things just for a picnic? He was afraid it wasn't going to be a picnic, after all. . . . The car suddenly turned into a wood, went for a few yards along a sort of cart-track, and stopped.

"Might as well do the other job now," said one man tersely. "It's just here."

The other took out a handkerchief and mopped his brow.

"Cripes! I've had about enough for one night."

"Don't be a fool. This one's child's play. The girl's going to let us in. It'll be over in a few minutes. Come on. Leave the other stuff here. It'll be as safe as if it was in the bank. Come on. . . . "

They got down from the seat and set off together in the direction of the road they had just left. William sat up at the back among Lady Markham's Georgian silver and considered the situation. It was, indeed, very far from being a picnic. The men were criminals—and the sort of criminals who'd stop at nothing. The courage that had upheld him in his conflicts with imaginary criminals began to ebb away. These weren't imaginary criminals. . . . They were, on the other hand, very real criminals. They'd think nothing of killing him when they found him in their car.

He wondered whether to get out of the car and hide in the wood, but suppose they came back and saw him in the act of getting out. . . . They'd kill him then, for certain. On the other hand, if he stayed in the car till they came back they were just as likely to kill him. It seemed to him that he was pretty certain to get killed whatever he did. He sighed pathetically. P'raps Robert and Ethel would be sorry they'd been so rotten to him then. Yes, he rather liked to think of the feelings of Robert and Ethel on receiving the news of his death. His father and mother would feel pretty mean about some things, too—not to speak of some of the masters at school. Yes, ole Monkey-face would be sorry he'd made such a fuss over a few rotten Latin verbs, and ole Markie, the headmaster, would have a few things on his conscience, too. . . . They'd all be sorry they'd been so rotten to him. Still—that thought, comforting in a way, did not really reconcile him to the prospect of an immediate encounter with two desperate criminals. Perhaps the best thing would be to make a dash for it and hide in the wood. He raised his head cautiously in the direction in which the men had gone. The coast seemed to be clear. The men did not seem to be returning. . . .

As a matter of fact, the men were returning, but by a different path from the one they had gone by, and the first sight that met their eyes on their return was that of a policeman's helmet rising slowly from the back of the car. They whipped behind a thick bush out of its range of vision.

"Cripes!" panted one. "A cop!"

"And I left my gun behind!" said the other.

"Don't be a fool," said the first. "What good would a gun be? D'you think there's only one of 'em? There was probably a car full of 'em following us. They'll be posted all over the wood. Let's drop the stuff and get out while there's time."

"But——"

"Come on, you fool. D'you want to be taken with it on you?"

They put the case behind the bush and crept noiselessly away, out of the wood and out of the story. . . .

William climbed from the car, and looked about him. A large bush nearby seemed to offer a convenient shelter from which he could take stock of the situation. He crept behind it and crouched for a minute or so in silence. Then—his gaze rested on the ground by his feet, and his eyes opened wide in surprise. A leather case lay on the road just in front of him. He picked it up and unfastened it, and his eyes opened wider still. A miniature Aladdin's cave of diamonds, pearls, and emeralds gleamed at him.

For a moment he was deprived even of the power of thought. Cars full of silver teapots and things, leather suit-cases full of jewels. . . . The only possible explanation, of course, was that he was dreaming. Things like this couldn't possibly happen in real life. He was sorry that it was a dream, because of the policeman's helmet. He did want to feel that he'd worn a policeman's helmet in real life—not just in a dream. He didn't mind about the teapots or the jewels, but he did mind about the policeman's helmet. The more he thought about it, however, the surer he was that it was a dream. It couldn't be anything else. Alone in a wood in the middle of the night with a lot of silver teapots and jewels. Stood to reason it was a dream. He'd probably be waking up any moment now, so he might as well make the most of it while it lasted. He needn't be afraid of those two men. It didn't matter what happened to you in a dream, because you'd wake up in the middle or it would all turn into something else as it so often did. He'd better make the most of being in a wood in a policeman's helmet before he found himself in a crowded tram-car in his pyjamas or something like that. He'd go back to the road and walk along there for a bit. He'd probably find something pretty queer. One always did in dreams.

He picked up the case, came from behind the bush, and hurried down the cart-track to the road. He'd better be quick or he'd be waking up, and he didn't want to do that till he'd had a bit more fun out of the dream. He reached the road and looked up and down it. It was empty. That was something of a disappointment. Still, he'd once had a dream in which an ordinary road had suddenly turned into a sea full of whales and pirates' ships while he was walking on it. Hopefully, he began to walk down the road, but it remained a road. This dream, he decided, was one of the sort that starts better than it goes on.

He reached a gate leading to a big house behind some trees. The windows were lighted up. He'd go up to it, walk straight in and see what happened. It didn't matter what one did in a dream. . . . Once he'd walked into a house in a dream (it had seemed quite an ordinary house) and found a lot of lions and tigers playing musical chairs. He walked up the drive to the front door, meaning to open it and walk straight in, or, if it was locked, to ring and see who came to it. A pirate or a wild animal or anything might come to it. But the door was open, and a lady stood in the hall with a policeman. She looked tearful and distraught.

"I've only found out quite by chance," she said. "Ordinarily I shouldn't have looked in that drawer again to-day. . . . Yes, *everything's* gone. The jewel-case broken open and *everything* gone. My diamonds and pearls and emeralds. . . . "

William stepped into the hall and handed her the case he carried.

"Are these the ones?" he said.

She snatched at the case and tore it open.

"Oh, yes . . . " she sobbed. "Yes, they are . . .

they're all here. Oh, how can I ever thank you?"

"Here," said the policeman, looking down in amazement at the diminutive figure, crowned so incongruously

"HOW DID *YOU* GET HOLD OF THEM?" ASKED THE POLICEMAN. "AND WHERE DID YOU GET THAT HELMET?"

by the majestic headgear of the force. "Here! How did *you* get hold of 'em?"

"Never mind how he got hold of them," said the stout lady. "He's brought them back to me. He's brought them back to me. . . . "

The policeman took out a notebook.

"Tell me your name and where you live and be quick about it, 'cause we've just been rung up over another job at Marleigh Manor. All their silver's been pinched."

"I've got that, too," said William carelessly. "I've got it in a car in the wood just across the road."

It was the policeman's turn to think that all this must be a dream. It couldn't—it *couldn't* be really happening. His jaw dropped open as he gazed down at the amazing little figure that met his look with an assured stare beneath the large and precariously balanced rim of its policeman's helmet.

"W-w-what?" he gasped. "S-s-s-say it again."

"Didn't you hear?" said William coldly. "I said I'd got all the silver in a car in the wood across the road."

"Well, I'll be blowed!" said the policeman weakly.

His notebook fell to the ground, and he did not feel quite steady enough to pick it up.

\* \* \*

A few minutes later William was interviewing Ronald Markham over the telephone.

"I say," stammered Ronald. "I—I can't tell you how marvellous we think it was of you. Anything you like in return, of course, we'd be only too glad to . . . "

William cocked his policeman's helmet to a more jaunty angle.

"Oh, that's all right," he said easily. "I mean—I've got it."

# Chapter 6

# William the Reformer

"Now, dear," said the Vicar's wife briskly, "I want you to listen to me very carefully. . . . "

She had called on Mrs. Brown in order to ask her if William might join the S.E.F.C.R.C. (Society for Educating Future Citizens in the Responsibilities of Citizenship), a society she had just started for the juvenile members of the village. Mrs. Brown was out, and so William, lolling dispiritedly in a chair and surreptitiously sucking a humbug, was receiving the full blast of her eloquence.

"You see, dear boy," she continued, "when you're grown up, it's you who will govern the country."

William sat up, galvanised into sudden interest.

"Crumbs!" he said. "I didn't know that."

"Yes, dear boy," murmured Mrs. Monks, "and that's why we want to prepare you to govern it properly."

"Oh, I'll govern it properly all right," said William, "once I get a chance of governing it at all."

"But you *are* going to get a chance of governing it, dear," said Mrs. Monks. "You are actually going to govern it."

This idea was so surprising that William swallowed half his humbug unsucked. Evidently his fame had spread farther than he had realised.

"WHEN YOU'RE GROWN UP, MY DEAR BOY, IT'S YOU WHO
WILL GOVERN THE COUNTRY."
"CRUMBS!" SAID WILLIAM.

"Do you mean," he said, "that I've been chosen to
govern the country same as this Hitler an' Muss——
what's-his-name?"

"Well, not exactly, dear," admitted the Vicar's wife,
"but it comes to the same in the end. Yes, it certainly
comes to the same in the end. Yours will be a collective
responsibility instead of an individual one, but—yes, it's
just as solemn a responsibility as theirs."

"Crumbs!" breathed William, then added in a
business-like voice: "When do I start?"

"As soon as you're twenty-one, dear boy."

"Oh. . . . I don't mind startin' a bit before that," offered William. "I'll start to-morrow if they like. Shall I have a palace to live in?"

"I hope so, dear," said the Vicar's wife and quoted dreamily:

"'The mind is its own place, and in itself
Can make a hell of heaven, a heaven of hell.'"

"We can all live in palaces if we want to, dear boy."

This theory was a bit above William's head, but he gathered definitely that he would have a palace to live in when he was governing the country.

"Shall I have soldiers?" he demanded.

"Of course, dear. The army and the navy of the country will belong to you."

"Crumbs!" said William again.

He had often imagined himself dictator of the country, but never before had the position been definitely offered to him by a responsible grown-up person.

"So you see, dear," went on the Vicar's wife, "you must train yourself very carefully for the day when all this power will be put into your hands."

"Oh, that's all right," said William airily. "I bet I could govern a country without any trainin' or suchlike. An' I don't mind startin' now either. 'S no good keepin' everyone waitin' till I'm twenty-one. Things might've got into an awful mess by then, an', anyway, I'd be too old to do much if I waited till I was twenty-one."

"No, dear," murmured the Vicar's wife absently as she consulted the other names on her list. "Now is the training time. The training time for great responsibilities. . . . You'll come to our first meeting to-morrow afternoon, won't you? *That's* right. Good-bye for the present, dear."

When she had gone and William had recovered somewhat from the surprise of being thus elected dictator by a, presumably, admiring country (though this was nothing to the things that happened to him regularly in his dreams), he began to consider in detail what this position would entail. All the sweet shops would belong to him. All the toy shops. All the cake shops. All the firework shops. Crumbs! He'd have a lovely time. And he'd shut up all the schools. He'd do that first thing. . . .

The Vicar's wife hurried on to the next address on her list. She was a vague, well-meaning woman, always too much taken up with what she had to say herself to listen to what other people had to say. She thought that her first call had been quite satisfactory. William Brown had seemed to take a great interest in what she told him and had, indeed, responded to the idea with an enthusiasm that slightly surprised her, for she knew that, as a rule, William Brown was not a responsive child. She hurried on to her next visit. . . .

\* \* \*

The members of the S.E.F.C.R.C. met in the Church Room at the Vicarage and listened to the Vicar's wife's opening address.

"And now, children," she ended. "I want you to hold a little Parliament, just so that you shall know how it's done and take more interest when you hear of this or that bill being passed."

"I'm not goin' to have a Parliament at all when I'm governin' the country," said William.

"Don't be silly, dear," said the Vicar's wife. "You'll

have to have a Parliament. You elect the men you want
to represent you in Parliament. They're there to carry
out your wishes."

"You mean they've gotter do what I tell 'em?"
demanded William.

"Yes, dear. More or less," said Mrs. Monks vaguely.

"Oh, all right," said William. "I don't mind that sort
of Parliament. But they'll jolly well have to do as I tell
'em or I'll turn the army an' navy on to 'em. Do the
police have to do what I tell 'em, too?"

"Yes, dear. More or less," said Mrs. Monks. "The
police are the servants of the public, and you are a
member of the public. You are what we might call a
representative citizen."

"A what?" asked William.

"A representative citizen, dear."

"I don't mind what I am," said William, "as long as
they have to do what I tell 'em."

"And now let us consider the composition of Parliament," said Mrs. Monks brightly, and proceeded to
consider it at length.

"And now," she said again, "I want you children to
have a little Parliament of your own, so that you can see
how it works. Let us see, now. Who will be the
Speaker?"

"I'll be him," said William. "I'm jolly good at
speaking."

"The Speaker doesn't speak, dear," said Mrs. Monks
patiently. "I've just explained all that."

"Why's he called the Speaker, then, if he doesn't
speak?" demanded William, who had been too much
occupied with visions of world dominion (for he had
decided to extend his power far beyond the limits of his
own country) to listen to what she was saying.

"He just keeps order," said Mrs. Monks still more patiently.

"Well, I'll do that," said William. "I'll keep order all right. I'll punch their heads if they don't do what I tell 'em."

"No, dear, you can't do that," said Mrs. Monks, and proceeded to give another lengthy exposition of parliamentary procedure, from which William gathered, to his deep disgust, that the position of power she had offered him was a very negative one. He felt as indignant and outraged as if he had been betrayed and deserted by an ungrateful country. After all he'd done for it—keeping order in its boundaries, spreading its power to the farthest ends of the earth—to be treated like this! But Mrs. Monks was offering the post of Prime Minister, and William decided to climb down from his offended dignity and save what he could from the wreck of his ambitions. A Prime Minister wasn't a dictator, but he was the next best thing.

"I'll be him," he said and added anxiously: "*He* can speak, can't he?"

"Oh, yes, dear. The whole country looks to him for a lead."

"I'll give it a lead all right," William assured her.

After all, he thought, he could use the post as a stepping-stone to that of dictator, and, finally, world potentate. He felt reluctant to give up the position that had seemed so securely his a few moments ago. Mrs. Monks was distributing other official posts to the other members of the meeting.

"Now you're a Parliament, children," she said at last, impressively, "one of the noblest institutions of mankind. Every great reform in history, almost, has been brought about by Parliament. It was Parliament that abolished the slave trade, and——" she paused and tried to think of some other reform, but, not being able to, ended somewhat lamely, "well—er—as I said—abolished the slave trade. Now"—brightly—"I want you children to think of some badly needed reform such as abolishing the slave trade and to propose and discuss it among yourselves, and then vote on it, just as if you were a real Parliament. . . . Can anyone think of some badly needed reform?"

"Abolishing school," suggested William.

"No, dear, that's not a reform," said Mrs. Monks. "Try to think of something sensible."

"Free sweet shops," suggested William.

"No, dear," said Mrs. Monks. "That's financially unsound." Her gaze swept over the little group. "Haven't any of the others any suggestion to make?"

But no one had, so William tried again.

"Christmas every week," he suggested.

"No, William," snapped Mrs. Monks. "Your suggestions are very silly indeed. They aren't reforms at all."

"Well, what is a reform, then?" demanded William.

"Something that makes the world a better place, dear," said Mrs. Monks.

"Well, then, all those things I said *are* reforms," persisted William. "They'd all make the world a jolly sight better place. I can think of a lot more, too——"

"*No*, dear," said Mrs. Monks firmly. "Now I want someone else to suggest something. Something sensible. William Brown's suggestions are all so silly."

No one, however, had anything to say except William, who muttered sulkily: "Put all the grown-ups in the zoo an' let the animals out."

"That's not funny, William," said Mrs. Monks distantly.

"It wasn't meant to be," said William.

The Vicar's wife sighed. William Brown had seemed fairly intelligent at the beginning, but now he was making a nuisance of himself, as usual.

"Very well, children," she said briskly, "as none of you can think of any fresh reform to introduce I propose that you pretend that you live in the old dark days of slave-owning, and that you bring in a bill to abolish it and discuss the matter among yourselves, just as if you were so many Pitts and Wilberforces."

"Who were they?" asked William.

"Pitt and Wilberforce were the great statesmen of their day," replied Mrs. Monks.

"I'll be them, then," said William.

"You can't be both, dear."

"Yes, I can," replied William.

If he couldn't be a world dictator, at least he could be Pitt and Wilberforce.

Mrs. Monks sighed again. She often wished that the poets who wrote so beautifully about childhood had had to do with William Brown. She glanced at her watch.

"Now, children," she went on, "I'll leave you to yourselves for a few moments as I have several things to see to. When I come back I shall expect to find the discussion in full swing."

She flashed her bright encouraging smile at them and went out of the room.

"Now, I'm this Pitt an' Willforce man," began William as soon as the door closed on her, "an' I say you've all gotter stop keepin' slaves. An' if anyone says he won't I'll punch his head. Does anyone say he won't?"

No one did, and after a moment's pause William went on:

"That's all right, then. Now all the slaves are free."

"Well, it's all jolly silly," said a small bored boy at the back of the room. "Freein' slaves when there aren't any!"

"Yes, but we're pretendin' there are," explained William.

"Well, it's *silly*," persisted the small boy. "It's silly pretendin' there's slaves when there aren't any. I *said* it was goin' to be silly. I wouldn't 've come if my mother hadn't made me."

"But there *are* slaves," said another boy, a pale boy with an earnest expression and large spectacles. "There *are* slaves. I *know* there are."

"How?" said the others with interest.

"I heard a man talkin' about it in the street, an' a lot of people were listenin' to him, so I listened, too, an' he said that all the workers were slaves. He said they were wage slaves. He said that all servants an' suchlike were slaves."

"Well, we'll free *them*, then," said William. "That makes it a bit more interestin'." He assumed his oratorical manner. "I say all servants an' suchlike have gotter be free. They're slaves an' they've gotter be free." He looked round pugnaciously. "Anyone think they've *not* gotter be free?" No one answered so he concluded: "Well, that's all right. Now they're all free."

"How'll they know they're free?" asked the pale boy with spectacles, who was, evidently, of a literal turn of mind.

William had not considered this.

"I s'pose we'll have to tell 'em," he said.

"When?" said the boy with spectacles.

"Now," said William. "I'm sick of Parliaments anyway. Come on. Let's go out an' tell the slaves they're free."

The boredom of the members of Parliament vanished at this suggestion, and they surged out after William and began to walk down the road. Like William they were sick of Parliaments and welcomed the chance of action.

They marched along till they came to the lodge gates of the Hall.

"There's plenty of servants at the Hall," said the spectacled boy. "We ought to go in an' tell 'em they're free."

Something of the zeal for reform died away from the little group.

"S'pose we go on a bit an' come back later," suggested someone cautiously. "Anyway"—glancing at William—"it's him what set them free. If anyone ought to go in an' tell 'em, it's him."

"All right," said William. "I'm not afraid to go in an' tell 'em they're free."

"I bet you are."

"I bet I'm not."

"All right. Go in an' tell 'em."

"All right. I will."

"I bet you won't."

"I bet I will."

"All right. Go on an' do it."

"All right. I am doin', aren't I?"

With that William started to walk jauntily up the drive to the front door. When he reached the front door his jauntiness deserted him. He looked back at the gate. The rest of the Parliament still stood there gazing after him. Retreat with honour was clearly impossible. He summoned all his courage, lifted the big knocker and sounded it several times. The door opened with disconcerting suddenness, and Mr. Bott's butler stood on the threshold. Mr. Bott's butler was a man of powerful build and forbidding expression. He looked down at William as if he were some small and noxious insect.

"Well?" he said grimly. "What do you want?"

William's courage forsook him. He had opened his lips to say "I've come to tell you that you've been set free," but closed them abruptly.

"Well?" said the butler again, still more grimly.

He took a step forward as he spoke and seemed to grow visibly larger and more powerful.

"P-please," stammered William, "p-please can you tell me the right time?"

The butler took another step forward, this time with a menacing gesture, and William, without stopping to make further explanation, fled precipitately down the steps. The little group at the gate, seeing the menacing gesture, also fled. If there was going to be trouble they weren't going to be in it. The butler, having put to flight the small noxious insect, resumed his normal size, then vanished, slamming the door behind him.

William went thoughtfully down the drive. He was aware that the group at the gate had witnessed his ignominious defeat, and would be waiting farther down the road to taunt him with it. Like many another before him, he was realising that the way of the reformer is hard. After a moment's hesitation he decided to make his way cautiously round to the back door and see if he could come across any of the less important members of Mrs. Bott's staff to whom he could impart the glad tidings of their newly acquired freedom. He could then rejoin the Parliament on the road without losing face. (William had an almost Oriental dislike of losing face.) He would have fulfilled his boast and performed his mission. He could even devise some satisfactory explanation of the butler's behaviour. The man was in the pay of the slave traders, and had been furious to learn that the slaves were now free. Yes, that would do nicely. All he'd got to do now was to find some unimportant member of the staff, impart the good news, and rejoin his Parliament.

He made his way round, through the shrubbery, to the back of the house. The kitchen door was closed, and there seemed to be no one about. William remained concealed behind a laurel bush, awaiting developments. After a few minutes the back door opened, and a kitchen maid came out and shook a table-cloth. She was small and plump and circular—round eyes, round face, round mouth. She looked amiable and stupid, and not much older than William himself. Emboldened, William rose from the cover of his laurel bush and confronted her.

"I say," he said. "You're free."

She looked at him without any surprise, as if people rose from laurel bushes every day of her life to announce her freedom.

"You mean I can go?" she said in a matter-of-fact way.

"Yes," said William, slightly taken aback by her attitude.

"Did they say so?"

The deliberations of his Parliament were evidently more widely known than he had realised.

"Yes, they said so all right."

"Well, wait for me," said the girl, still displaying no surprise. "I won't be a minute."

With that she disappeared, closing the kitchen door.

William still felt somewhat disconcerted by her casual reception of the great news. He had expected surprise, curiosity, gratitude.

But he was interested also. He wondered why the girl

"I SAY," SAID WILLIAM, "YOU'RE FREE."

had gone away so abruptly without waiting for further details. Perhaps she had gone to fetch some present as a token of her gratitude. He'd wait till she came back, anyway. He was far too much interested in the situation to leave it as it was. Soon the girl re-appeared. She wore a coat and hat.

"Come on," she said briskly to William, and led the way down a narrow path through the shrubbery to a gate that opened on to the lane. They'd avoided the waiting Parliament, anyway, and of that William was rather glad. He'd just as soon not face the waiting Parliament till he'd got the whole story to tell them, and the story seemed only to be beginning.

"Come on, can't you?" said the girl impatiently, quickening her pace.

She evidently took it as a matter of course that William should accompany her.

"B-but where are we going?" asked the mystified William.

"Home, of course," said the girl shortly.

William was silent. Perhaps it was the custom for a freed slave to take his or her liberator home to receive the thanks of the home circle. It might be rather embarrassing. It might, indeed, be more than embarrassing. Though he was always completely carried away by whatever drama he happened to be enacting at the moment, he had an uncomfortable feeling that perhaps this girl had taken his announcement too seriously.

"What's your name?" said the girl.

William searched his memory for the elusive names Pitt and Wilberforce.

"Hole," he said at last uncertainly.

"Don't be silly," she said. "It can't be. No one's called Hole."

William was inclined to agree with her. People weren't called Hole. He'd try the other.

"Well, it's something that begins with Will an' ends with something you have for breakfast. Wait a minute. . . . I remember. . . . No, I don't. . . . Well, it's jus' that. It's something you have for breakfast. I'll remember it in a minute."

"Porridge," suggested the girl.

"I don't *think* it's porridge," said William.

"It mus' be," said the girl firmly. "If it's something you have for breakfast it mus' be Porridge. You couldn't be called Hamaneggs or Toast or Breadanbutter. It mus' be Porridge. It's a silly name, anyway. An' I never met anyone before that didn't know their name. You mus' be balmy." She examined him with dispassionate interest. "You *look* balmy."

"Balmy yourself!" said William coldly. He thought that her tone displayed a deplorable lack of gratitude to her benefactor.

"Come on, for goodness' sake," she went on. "We'll never get there if you dawdle along like this."

William's distaste for his protégée was increasing. He didn't know why he'd ever taken the trouble to free her. He wished now he'd left her a slave.

They were approaching a small farm house.

"Here we are," said the girl, and repeated her irritating "Come on, can't you?"

William accompanied her into a large kitchen with a stone floor, where a middle-aged woman stood tidying her hair at a mirror on the wall. She turned round as they entered. She held a comb in one hand and several hairpins in her mouth.

"Here's the boy, mother," said the girl, pointing to William. William assumed a bashful, self-conscious expression. Surely the parents of the freed slave, at any rate, would give him his due meed of honour and gratitude. But the woman merely looked him over without much interest, then, nodding to a farther door, said, through the hairpins: "All right. Go straight through."

William, not quite knowing what else to do, walked through this door, closing it carefully behind him. He found himself in a passage leading to an open door, beyond which could be seen part of the farmyard. He walked slowly and thoughtfully down this passage, thinking that never since the world began could any freer of slaves have been treated so oddly. Half-way down the passage he came to another open door, leading into a cheerful room where a fire was burning brightly. He looked in. It was empty. Empty of human beings, that is, but full of what was, to William, of far more interest than human beings. A large table stood in the middle of the room, literally covered with dainties of every kind, and, seeing it, William realised that it was a long time since he had had lunch and that he was very hungry.

He entered the room cautiously, closing the door behind him. And suddenly the explanation of the mystery came to him in a flash. It was to this room that he had been directed when told to go "straight through". This feast was prepared for him as a mark of gratitude. He was being fêted, as, indeed, was only right. Probably that man Hole, or whatever his name was, went round to the homes of the slaves he'd freed and was given feasts like this. It was jolly kind of them, and it looked a jolly good feast, and he might as well start on it straight away, so that they'd know he appreciated it. He'd finished a jelly, a trifle, a plate of biscuits, and had eaten half an iced cake, when the door opened, and a very old woman entered, leaning on a stick, followed by a lot of other people, including the freed slave and her mother. They stood staring at him with expressions of utter amazement, which changed to fury as they saw the depredations he had made among the provisions. In the short pregnant silence that followed William realised that he was not, as he had thought, the guest of honour at this feast, that he was, in fact, very far from being the guest of honour. He backed apprehensively as a large red-faced man advanced threateningly upon him. Then suddenly the old woman, who alone of the group had looked neither surprised nor angry, began to laugh.

"Who is he?" she said. "Where's he come from?"

"He's the thatcher's boy," answered the freed slave. "He's come to help his father with the barn roof. Aunt Flossie was going to ask Mrs. Bott at the Women's Institute meeting if I could come to Grandma's party——"

"I'm ninety-nine to-day, young man," put in the old lady proudly.

"—an' she was goin' to send me word by the thatcher's boy if I could, 'cause he was comin' here, anyway, to help his father with the barn roof an' he could come along with me an'——"

"What's he called?" said the old lady.

"He doesn't know," said the girl, "but he thinks he's called Porridge."

"But the thatcher's boy's here," said the red-faced man angrily. "He's here helping the thatcher on the barn roof. He said he called to tell our Ellen she could come, but she'd gone already." He flung an arm out angrily in William's direction. "Who *is* this boy? He comes in from nowhere and eats the whole tea up——"

"Nonsense!" put in the old lady tartly. "Martha

always provides twice as much as anyone can eat. The boy's eaten hardly anything."

"Who *is* he, that's what I want to know?" sputtered the red-faced man.

"He doesn't know himself, father," said the girl, "but he thinks his name's Porridge."

"I'll porridge him," said the man advancing threateningly upon William. "Who-are-you-and-what-are-you-doing-here?" he thundered fiercely.

"W-well," stammered William, "it's sort of like this. You see, I'm settin' slaves free so I set *her* free"— pointing to the girl—"an'——"

"What?" bellowed the man.

"I said he was balmy," said the girl triumphantly. "I knew he was, as soon as he said his name was Porridge."

"What's your name?" said the man to William with ominous distinctness.

"William."

"And what are you doing here?"

"He's come to my birthday party," said the old lady.

"Oh, has he?" said the man. "He hasn't been invited."

"Then I invite him now," said the old lady. "I like him. I want him to come. My first sweetheart was called William. He wasn't called William Porridge, of course, but the poor boy can't help his name. He's more to be pitied than blamed for it. People don't make their own names. Come an' sit by me, William, and tell me all about yourself. Now, George, stop looking so cross. I shall have whom I like to my birthday party. Have another piece of cake, William. It's very nice to see a fresh face. I'm sick to death of never seeing anyone but my relations, from week's end to week's end. . . . You're a little like *my* William, though he was handsomer, of course. He was fifteen and I was fourteen. I lived with an old aunt then, and we *did* play some tricks on her, I can tell you. One day we——"

She launched into a racy account of her childhood's

"WHAT ARE YOU DOING HERE?"

"HE'S COME TO MY BIRTHDAY PARTY," SAID THE OLD LADY.
"I INVITE HIM NOW."

escapades, to which William, who had taken his seat next to her, listened with interest.

Ellen hovered about him, plying him with food, obviously fascinated by the mystery of his personality. "Porridge," she muttered to herself, "slaves . . . balmy. . . . "

The irascible George had shrugged his shoulders and dismissed the matter temporarily from his mind. He didn't know where the wretched boy had come from or what he was doing here, but the old lady had taken a fancy to him, so one couldn't do anything about it. Not while the old lady was there anyway. So he dismissed the matter from his mind and discussed farming prospects with his relations.

His wife hurried to and from the kitchen, repairing the depredations that William had made in the feast.

The old lady continued to pour out spicy reminiscences of her youth.

William sat listening with interest, but managing at the same time to make an excellent tea.

He was aware that the moment of reckoning with the red-faced man was yet to come, but, with luck, even that might be evaded. Meantime he was enjoying the tea, the old lady's reminiscences and the obvious interest of the freed slave.

He was, in fact, feeling, as probably most social reformers feel in their brighter moments, that all the trouble he had taken was being amply repaid. . . .

# Chapter 7

# St. Mars' Day

The Outlaws stood in a row, their faces pressed against the shop window, gazing at the display of crimson hearts, cupids, and mincing maids and gallants within.

"Aren't they sickenin'?" said William at last, in a voice of heartfelt disgust.

"They're Valentines," explained Henry.

"It's St. Valentine's day to-morrow," added Ginger.

"Well, I think all that soppy stuff oughter to be put a stop to," said William sternly. "Who was he, anyway?"

He appealed to Henry, who had a reputation for omniscience among his contemporaries. The drawback to such a reputation is that its owner never likes to admit himself ignorant on any point whatsoever.

"Oh . . . he was jus' a sort of saint," said Henry vaguely.

William's eyes returned to the display of hearts and cupids.

"Funny sort of saint," he commented. "What did he do—'sides drawin' soppy pictures, I mean?"

"He didn't do anything else," said Henry. "The pictures took him all his time."

"Well, I'm jus' about *sick* of it," said William. "Year after year of it. There's some sense in Guy Fawkes and Shrove Tuesday an' Christmas an' the others, but this——! I've a good mind to put a stop to it myself."

They began to walk slowly down the road.

"How could you?" demanded Douglas after a slight silence.

"I've not thought about it yet," said William, "but I bet I jolly well could, once I began thinkin' about it."

"Well, go on. Begin thinkin' about it," challenged Ginger.

There was another silence, during which William evidently began thinking about it.

"Well, I'd start somethin' else instead," he said at last.

"What?" demanded the others simultaneously.

"Give me time to *think*," said William irritably. "You keep on an' on an' on at me without givin' me time to *think*. Even the King's gotter think some time."

"All right," said Ginger soothingly. "Well, go on. Think."

William thought, while the others watched him expectantly.

"Well, I'd start a different sort of saint," he said, after a pause. "An opposite sort of saint." He looked at Henry. "Who's the saint of war?"

"Mars," said Henry promptly.

"Well, I'd turn it into a St. Mars' day 'stead of a St. Valentine's day. It'd be the day when everyone could have as many fights with their enemies as they wanted to, and no one could stop them. Yes, that's a jolly good idea. Better than these sickenin' cards. People fightin' with their enemies all over the place." In imagination he watched the sight. It obviously cheered him. "Yes, that'd be a jolly good idea. Everyone fightin' their enemies all over the place, all day. Shouldn't wonder if it didn't turn out almost as much fun as Guy Fawkes' day."

"The police'd stop 'em fightin'," said Douglas.

"No, they wouldn't. Not when I've got things goin' prop'ly. I'd have all the police shut up for that day."

"Where?"

"Somewhere big. Crystal Palace or somewhere like that. It'd be quite fun for them, too. They could look out of the windows an' watch the people fightin'. Or they could fight each other. It's a jolly good idea, I think."

"Yes, it is," agreed Ginger, "but how'd you start it?"

"Well, everythin's got to start gradual," said William. "Someone jus' starts it an' then it sort of spreads. If we start it ourselves, I bet it'll spread jolly quick. . . ."

"How'll we start it?" demanded Douglas.

"We'll just start fightin' our enemies," said William simply, "an' I bet everyone else'll start fightin' theirs, an' soon that old Valentine person'll be quite forgotten."

"When will we start it?" asked Douglas somewhat apprehensively. Douglas was always slightly less ready than the others to assimilate a new idea.

"We'll start first thing to-morrow," said William.

"They start to-night," Ginger reminded him. "They send out these soppy Valentine cards to-night."

"Then we'll start to-night," said William. "We'll send out Mars' cards."

Half an hour later the Outlaws sat on the floor of William's bedroom organising the campaign.

"First thing we've gotter do," said William, "is to make out a list of enemies, then we'll know who to start on. Tell you what. Let's not put an awful lot of enemies down. Let's save some up for nex' year. Let's jus' put three or four down an' do them prop'ly. Anyone got any paper?"

No one had, so William tore the two middle pages out of his arithmetic book, a thing he had already done so often that the arithmetic master (who fancied himself as a wit) had waxed sarcastic on the subject.

"It's losing weight almost visibly, Brown," he had said, with mock concern. "I think you ought to give it a tonic."

"I say, you'll get into an awful row if you pull any more pages out of that book, after what he said," Ginger warned him.

"No, I won't," retorted William, who had a sound, if rudimentary, knowledge of human nature. "He liked that joke about a tonic so much that he'll be jolly glad to get a chance to use it again. Come on. Let's go on with the list."

The name of Hubert Lane took its place naturally at the head of the list. Hubert Lane, a fat sly boy of about William's age, pampered by an adoring mother, the leader of a gang of kindred spirits whom he attached to himself by largesse of doughnuts and ginger-beer, had been the enemy of the Outlaws from time immemorial. Lately the feud had waned somewhat, not from any lack of enmity on either side, but because the two factions had not happened to see much of each other, owing to Hubert's having been kept home with a series of colds. Hubert's colds were his mother's chief activity during the winter months. She dosed him daily with remedies and preventatives, never let him go out without a chest-protector and a muffler, and couldn't understand why he caught so many. . . . But, just at present, Hubert was in the stage (always a short one) between his last cold and his next, and so the Outlaws felt that the stage was well set for Mars' day.

"Yes," said William, writing down the name with

satisfaction, "it would have been a pity if he'd had one of his colds jus' now."

The Outlaws by no means invariably came off victors in their struggles with the Hubert Laneites, for Hubert Lane was possessed of a cunning and duplicity that amply compensated for his lack of physical prowess.

"Well, who'll we put down next?" said William, licking the almost invisible point of his pencil in readiness for his next entry.

"Ole Markie," said Ginger.

They looked at him doubtfully. The headmaster, like Hubert Lane, was their natural enemy, and Ginger had only recently incurred his Olympian displeasure, but . . .

"We couldn't fight *him*," objected Douglas, voicing their doubts.

"N-no," agreed William, "but—well, he's an enemy all right."

"Yes, he jolly well *is*," said Ginger bitterly, "an' I don't see why we shouldn't try'n score off him some way. If we only put down people we can axshully fight, then we can't put down any grown-ups at all, an' I jolly well think we've got more grown-up enemies than any other sort."

"All right," said William. "We'll count scorin' off grown-ups as well as fightin' boys. Yes, that oughter make it all jolly excitin'. Now, who'll we have next?"

"Mrs. Monks," said Ginger. "I'm sick of havin' to go to meetin's an' listen to her talkin' about Parliaments an' things."

"All right," said William. "Yes, we'll put her down. I had a jolly good tea over that slave business, but she took away my caterpillar, jus' 'cause I was teachin' it to walk along my pencil when she was tellin' us about someone called the Leak of Nations, an' I bet she's not rememberin' to feed it reg'ly. Yes, we'll put her down all right. Who'll we put next?"

"I think that'll do for one day," suggested Douglas.

"It's only three," said William.

"Yes, but they're sort of hard ones," said Douglas.

William considered the list in silence for a moment.

"Yes, they are," he admitted at last. "They're hard ones all right. Perhaps they'll do for this year."

"There's the Mars cards to do, too," Henry reminded them. "Who'll we send them to?"

"Jus' the people on the list," said William. "We'll always send Mars cards to the ones we're goin' to fight an' score off on St. Mars' day."

"Can't we have somethin' to eat with it?" said Ginger.

"What do you mean?"

"Well, same as pancakes on Shrove Tuesday an' parkin on Guy Fawkes' day an' turkey at Christmas."

"No," said William firmly. "That ole Valentine did without anythin' to eat, so Mars must, too. Come on. Let's do the cards."

The cards necessitated a certain amount of preparation. Correspondence cards and envelopes had to be filched from Mrs. Brown's bureau, and red ink from Robert's bedroom. When finished, however, they were certainly impressive. Black skulls, surrounded by red cross-bones, bore the legend, in black and red letters alternately: BEWEAR. The Outlaws gazed at them admiringly.

"Well," said William, "it's a jolly sight better than all those hearts an' suchlike what that ole Valentine has. I bet in—say, two years—there won't be a single

Valentine card in the world. Everyone'll be havin' Mars cards instead.''

They addressed the envelopes, put on the stamps (also filched from Mrs. Brown's desk), and took them out to post. On the way they learnt an important piece of news. Mrs. Lane was giving a Valentine party to-morrow for Hubert. There were to be an equal number of little boys and little girls, and the games were to be Kiss in the Ring, Postman's Knock, Turn the Trencher, Forfeits, and others of similar kind.

"Crumbs!" said William thoughtfully. "We·ought to be able to do something about that. We'll have a jolly good try anyway."

His mind was busy on the subject all that evening. The situation held possibilities that made indiscriminate street fighting seem crude in comparison. Besides, meeting Hubert Lane in open warfare generally had unpleasant consequences, for Hubert always complained to his parents, and his parents then complained to the parents of the aggressors, who generally exacted vengeance from their offspring for the sake of peace. No, something far more subtle might be evolved from the Hubert Lane Valentine party.

"We'll jolly well manage to turn it into a Mars party somehow," said William to the Outlaws on their way to school. "We'll have to have a jolly good think about it."

They thought about it during morning school to such effect that every one of them was kept in for inattention, but still no suitable plan of campaign occurred to them.

"I'll make it a holiday when I've got it goin' prop'ly," said William, feelingly, "then we'll have a bit of time to think. I'll make 'em all holidays, Shrove Tuesday, Guy Fawkes' day, Leap Year, Mars' day and all of 'em.

*School* on *Mars'* day!" he ejaculated in disgust. "It ought to be stopped by lor."

He gleaned a cheering piece of news, however, on the way home to lunch. Seeing Mrs. Lane talking to a friend just outside the village shop, he hung about, pretending to be absorbed by the contents of the shop window, in order to overhear what she said.

"Yes," she was saying, "I'm having a little Valentine party for Huby this afternoon. Such a pretty idea, I think, don't you? Oh, no, I'm not going to be there. The little laddies and girlies are to be left entirely to themselves. *Much* more fun for them, I think, don't you? Besides, Huby's a perfect little host. He doesn't need any help from anyone."

It was a great relief to know that Mrs. Lane was not to be there. William hastened to impart the news to his Outlaws as quickly as possible.

"Tell you what," went on William, struck by an idea, "let's hold 'em up."

"Hold 'em up?" repeated Ginger, mystified.

"Yes, same as they do in America. They're always holdin' 'em up there. Parties an' suchlike. They jus' go in with pistols an' say, 'stick 'em up' an' they stick 'em up, scared as anythin'. It mus' be true 'cause I've seen it on the pictures."

"He'll only tell his mother an' there'll be another row," said Douglas.

"No, we'll wear masks," said William. "They always wear masks on the pictures. I've gotter mask I had in a cracker at Christmas. An' those who haven't got masks can have black handkerchiefs tied over their eyes."

"All my handkerchiefs are white," said Ginger, taking one out of his pocket. "At least," he added, looking at it, "they are when they've been washed."

"Well, you can black one, can't you?" said William impatiently. "What's ink for?" No one answered this rhetorical question, so he continued. "I'll try'n' find another mask. I think Robert's got one. He had one out of the crackers same as me, an' I bet he's got it put away somewhere. I'll have a look through his things. I've gotter pistol an' Ginger's got an air-gun. What've you others got?"

Henry did not possess pistol or air-gun, but suggested taking the hammer and saw from his new carpenter's set. William objected to these weapons on the ground that they were unsuitable for a hold-up, and persuaded him to substitute for them the largest cannon from his toy fort, which, he reminded him, was "nearly as big as a small pistol". Douglas was torn between a patent gas-stove lighter (from the kitchen) and a small hearth-brush (from his mother's bedroom), either of which, he said, held in a certain way, exactly resembled a pistol. In the end he decided on the hearth-brush.

Just before they separated, William had another inspiration and told them all to "borrow" raincoats and hats from the adult members of their households in order to make their appearance more impressive and mature.

"We'll just go in sudden, same as they do on the pictures," he said, "an' say, 'stick 'em up.' I bet they'll be scared all right."

There was a silence, during which each of them saw four sinister figures appear suddenly in a crowded room, heard a gasp of horror, saw a terrified group of revellers holding up trembling hands. It was a highly gratifying picture.

"What'll we do then?" said Henry suddenly.

They were slightly disconcerted by the question. No

one had thought of that. The glorious moment of the hold-up had dwarfed both present and future in their minds. "Oh, well——" began William and ended lamely, "well—what do they do on the pictures?"

"They make 'em do whatever they want 'em to do," said Henry.

"Tell you what," said Ginger. "We'll make 'em promise never to be Valentines any more. We'll jus' tell 'em about Mars an' make 'em promise always to keep Mars' day 'stead of Valentine's, all the rest of their lives. We'll tell 'em we'll shoot 'em dead if they don't."

"Yes, that's a jolly good idea," said William. "Well, come on. Let's go'n' get the things."

It was an impressive quartet that met outside the Lanes' house about quarter of an hour later. Each wore a raincoat much too big for him and a hat that came down so far over his eyes that it almost hid his mask. Black streaks down Ginger's face and large black spots on his collar testified to the fact that he had taken William's advice as to the manufacture of a mask, but had allowed insufficient time for the handkerchief to dry. William, impressive in his black domino, held his pistol high up against his shoulder in what he imagined to be true desperado fashion. Ginger, who was rather truculent as a result of having swallowed large quantities of ink, made savage passes with his air-gun on all sides. Henry's mask, a piece of black velvet ribbon found in his family's rag bag, had slipped down from his eyes and kept getting in his mouth, while Douglas, in a moment of inspiration, had hurriedly burnt a cork in his bedroom just before coming out, and given himself a ferocious moustache, an inch thick, that reached to his eyebrows. He felt that this counter-balanced the slight ignominy of the hearth-brush pistol.

William's gaze rested on them proudly. To his, perhaps biased, eye they looked as noble a band of desperadoes as had ever been seen, fit devotees, indeed, of their patron, Mars.

WILLIAM LOOKED PROUDLY ON HIS FEROCIOUS GANG.

"Come on," he said. "We'll go very slow through the garden an' look in at the window to see what they're doin' before we burst in on 'em."

They crept through the side gate of the Lanes' garden, then slipped suddenly behind a small summer-house and "froze". Four people were coming down the garden path—Hubert Lane and three of his friends. They were whispering and giggling together. The Outlaws could just see them. They wore their Eton suits. Their patent-leather shoes gleamed in the dusk. They entered the summer-house. William had already noticed that there was a bolt on the outside of the summer-house door. A sudden idea struck him. If these four were imprisoned here, the rest of the party would be easier to deal with. In any case, the temptation to slam and bolt the door and imprison his enemy was too strong to be resisted. He communicated this plan by signs to the others, and in a moment it was neatly effected, the door slammed, the bolt run home . . . then the Outlaws crept silently towards the house. Muffled cries followed them.

"I say, who did that?" "I say, don't try to be funny." "Go on . . . let us out now." The voices were only slightly indignant. Evidently Hubert and his friends imagined the outrage to be a joke played on them by one of the other guests, and did not expect it to last long.

The Outlaws crept towards the brightly lit room where the party was evidently being held. The blinds were drawn, so that it was impossible to see what was going on inside. One of the windows was a French window. Very cautiously William tried the handle. It was loose. He marshalled his force around him, then suddenly flung it open, pulled aside the curtains, and stood with his pistol pointing into the room.

"Stick 'em up," he said in a gruff voice.

"Stick 'em up," repeated the Outlaws, taking their places beside him. (Ginger somewhat spoilt the effect of his entrance by tripping over his raincoat.) Four little girls looked at them in surprise. The Outlaws themselves were taken aback. The party was evidently of smaller dimensions than they had imagined. It had not, in fact, been popular, and the majority of the invitations had been refused. Hubert and his three friends were the only representatives of their sex.

"Stick 'em up," said William again, intensifying the gruffness of his tone in order to hide his dismay.

The little girls, however, didn't look at all frightened. They were gazing at the grotesque newcomers in unaffected delight.

"Oh, *lovely*!" said a little girl with red curls, clapping her hands. "That's a *lovely* surprise."

She pulled off William's hat and mask, then gave a start.

"Why, it's not Hubert," she said. "It's a different boy."

"It's William Brown," said a little girl with long fair ringlets. "I know it's William Brown 'cause my mother's often told me not to play with him."

William raised his pistol again.

"Stick 'em up," he said, but in a voice that sounded uncertain, even to himself. No one, however, was taking any notice of him. The four little girls were pulling the hats, masks, ribbons and dyed handkerchief from the Outlaws' heads with screams of excitement.

"They're all new boys," said the little girl with ringlets. "What a *lovely* surprise! Hubert and the others said they were going to give us a surprise, but we didn't know it was going to be such a lovely surprise as this. Isn't it *fun*? Have *you* got a Valentine party, too, and have you changed places with Hubert for the second part of it? I think it's a lovely idea. . . . "

"Well, come on," said the little girl with red hair. "Let's start another game."

"Listen to me," said William earnestly, "you've all gotter promise . . . "

But no one was listening to him. Two of the little girls

"STICK 'EM UP!" SAID WILLIAM.

were quarrelling shrilly as to what game they should
play, and the other two were pointing Douglas's hearth-
brush at him and saying "stick 'em up".

"Turn the Trencher."

"No, we played that last. Postman's Knock."

"*No*. Forfeits."

"Listen," implored William again. "*Listen*. This is
St. Mars' day an' . . . "

"LOVELY!" SAID A LITTLE GIRL. "THAT'S A LOVELY
SURPRISE."

But still no one listened.

The Outlaws stood helpless, looking to William for a
lead.

"Listen," said William yet again, hoarse with
urgency. "Listen. I want to tell you all about this St.
Mars an' . . . "

"Turn the Trencher," said the little girl with red hair,
triumphantly.

She seized a wooden trencher from a corner of the room and spun it round.

"William Brown," she called.

So imperious was her voice that William automatically leapt forward to catch the spinning circle.

"Go on," she said. "Turn it and call someone's name."

William obeyed. Small as she was, there was that in her voice that had to be obeyed.

The game went on for five or ten minutes. Ginger, Henry, Douglas, despite themselves, obeyed the little girl's commands, leaping forward to retrieve the falling trencher, spinning it, and calling out a name.

"Now Postman's Knock," called out the little girl, who had appointed herself mistress of the ceremonies.

"No," protested William, "you've *gotter* listen. Listen. This is all wrong. It's Mars we've gotter——"

"William Brown go out first," ordered the little girl with red hair.

William Brown went out.

Postman's Knock was even more humiliating than Turn the Trencher.

The Outlaws avoided meeting each other's eyes, even at one point tried to sneak out of the French window again, but were recalled sharply by the little girl with red hair.

Followed Forfeits, at which William had to walk round the room on his hands and knees, Ginger to Maiow like a cat, Henry sing "Twinkle, Twinkle, Little Star," and Douglas repeat his twice times table. And the little girl's authority seemed to grow more and more hypnotic. They didn't know why they obeyed. They obeyed sheepishly, unwillingly, but still they obeyed. Their spirit was broken. The dreadful evening wore on. The little girl with red hair put on a gramophone record

and announced a dance. She danced with William. The
others danced with Henry, Douglas and Ginger. Dispiritedly, ashamedly, the Outlaws trailed round the
room with their partners. The whole thing was a night-
mare. Suddenly there came the sound of voices. The
shouts of the Hubert Laneites had, at last, attracted
notice, and they had been rescued by Mrs. Lane.
Accompanied by her, they were making their way back
to the house. Their voices rose in angry expostulation,
Mrs. Lane's in indignant sympathy.

"Someone locked us in."

"Who did, darling?"

"I don't know. If I did I'd jolly well——"

"We'll try to find out, darling. I'll talk to father about
it and we'll——"

Quick as lightning the Outlaws slipped to the French
window and vanished into the night. They ran till they
had reached a safe distance from the house, then faced
each other gloomily.

"Well!" said Ginger, and repeated more eloquently,
*"Well!"*

"What about that ole Mars you were goin' to start?"
demanded Douglas indignantly.

"Well, I couldn't help it, could I?" said William
bitterly. "Why din't the rest of you do somethin',
anyway?"

"What *could* we do?" said Ginger.

"Well, what could I do?" countered William. "If I'd
known there was goin' to be girls I'd never have gone
there. I could have fought any amount of boys."

"An' we've not even started on ole Markie an' Mrs.
Monks."

"We'd better put them off till next year," said
Douglas hastily.

"Well, I think," said Ginger, "that if that ole Mars an' Valentine——"

"Oh, shut up," said William. "I'm sick of 'em both. Let's go home to bed."

# Chapter 8

# Uncle Charlie and the Outlaws

William walked slowly down the road, dragging his toes in the mud—a proceeding that always afforded him a certain obscure pleasure, which was enhanced by the knowledge that if any of his family were present they would at once stop it. To-day the pleasure he derived from it was a sub-conscious one, for his thoughts were elsewhere. A master at school had recently divulged the fact, hitherto unsuspected by William, that March was the month of Mars, the God of War. The subject had painful associations for William. Only last month he had tried to change St. Valentine's day, of which he strongly disapproved, into Mars' day, which he thought could not fail to provide excitement, but without success. The memory of the failure still rankled. Failure, indeed, seemed to have pursued him lately. He had started a Punishment Insurance Society at school. The members were to pay him a penny a week and to receive twopence for a detention and threepence for a caning. He had thought it all out, and it had seemed an excellent scheme, but it had been unfortunately discovered by Authority, and all its members punished, so that it was now bankrupt and discredited.

An outbreak of measles had next seemed to afford a

diversion from the general monotony of life, but, despite all his efforts, he had not succeeded in catching it. As a last resort he had manufactured a rash on his face with the help of Ethel's lipstick, which had so alarmed his mother that she had sent for the doctor, but the doctor had made short work of it, and he had been summarily despatched to school. Altogether, things had not been going well with him, and he was in a fit state of mind to enlist himself once more as a desperado under the banner of Mars. It was half-way through March, too. There was no time to waste. Pity he hadn't known about it before. Well, he must find an enemy quickly and start on him—or her—or them—at once.

He considered his own family. They were, of course, his natural enemies, but his feud with them was a perennial affair of larger scope than could possibly be confined to one month. Half its pleasure would be gone were it to be thus localised. The Hubert Laneites? They, too, were a more or less perennial affair, though it wouldn't be a bad idea to intensify the feud just for March. It had dragged on indecisively long enough. But it would be better to make a completely new enemy and finish the whole thing off in the appropriate month. He just felt like a new enemy, too. It would be a definite focus on which to direct all his vague sense of grievance against Fate. He grew tired of dragging his toes in the mud and, climbing up on to a stile by the roadside, sat there, considering the situation, and throwing stones absently at the neighbouring trees.

People passed along the road. Some greeted him, some ignored him, some (especially those who became chance targets of badly aimed stones) reproached him. He gazed at them with lofty contempt. He knew them—knew where they lived, what they did, who their children were. He wasn't sufficiently interested in them even to want them for enemies. He wished that someone he'd never seen before would come down the road, someone obviously so objectionable as to be the perfect enemy. No sooner had the wish formed itself in his mind than a man appeared, walking along the road from the direction of the station.

He was a large man with a very check suit, a very black moustache, and a very complacent expression. He carried a suit-case. William's face brightened as he looked

HE WAS A LARGE MAN, WITH A VERY CHECK SUIT AND A
BLACK MOUSTACHE.

at him. He would, on the whole, have preferred someone of his own age, he even felt a slight regret at abandoning the Hubert Laneites, but there was no doubt that this was the perfect enemy. The newcomer ignored him, walking on down the road with a rolling, self-important strut. As William gazed after him, his mind busy with the possibilities of the situation, he was suddenly precipitated on to the ground by a sharp attack from behind. Picking himself up and glaring angrily from a mud-covered face, he saw his recently elected enemy standing in the road doubled up with laughter, surrounded by a crowd of giggling Hubert Laneites. William started forward pugnaciously, then stopped, for not only was he many times outnumbered, but the newcomer carried a stout stick.

"Doesn't he look *funny*, Uncle Charlie?" said Hubert Lane, holding his sides with laughter.

Then they all turned and went on down the road with the newcomer. William gazed after them thoughtfully. He remembered now hearing that Mrs. Lane's brother was coming to stay with them. The situation became clear. Hubert Lane and his friends had walked across the fields to meet Hubert's uncle and, creeping up behind him while he sat on the stile, had attacked him, with characteristic lack of sportsmanship, in the rear. William went home, washed, then set out to meet his Outlaws, to whom he explained the situation with his accustomed eloquence.

"You see, this month belongs to Mars what's the God of War, an' we've gotter *do* something about it. We made an awful mess of turnin' Valentine into Mars, so this sort of gives us another chance. I think we *oughter* do something about it. We oughter find a good enemy an' start on him straight away. Well, this man's a jolly good enemy. An' he's got Hubert Lane an' the others with him, so we can have a real go at them all together."

But this proved more difficult than William had thought it would. It was not that Uncle Charlie ignored the feud. He adopted it, indeed, so readily as to make it peculiarly his own. He had what Hubert Lane's mother called "the heart of a boy", and he threw himself into all the Hubert Laneites' activities with untiring zest. His great boyish laugh rang out as he romped about the garden with them or distributed among them the bars of chocolate cream they loved. He referred to himself as "Charlie Pan, the boy who wouldn't grow up." Some people thought him charming and some didn't.

The Outlaws, of course, belonged to the latter class. They would have ignored him if they hadn't chosen him as their enemy, and if he had been content to ignore them. But the Hubert Laneites' feud appealed to what he called the "eternal boy" in him, and he pursued it indefatigably. He even climbed up a tree that grew in the Lanes' garden and overhung the road, in order to throw a bucket of water over the Outlaws as they passed beneath. More by good luck than good management, most of it fell on William. . . .

To make matters worse Uncle Charlie had managed to acquaint himself with most of the misfortunes that had lately befallen William and the Outlaws, and would call out derisive references to the insurance scheme or to William's "measles" from the Lanes' garden as they passed down the road on the other side of the hedge.

When this had gone on for a few weeks, William and the Outlaws held a meeting to consider the situation.

"If only we could *do* somethin'," said William, dispiritedly.

"What *can* we do?" demanded Ginger. "It's makin'

'em too cocky for words. They're getting awful."

"We'll be able to fix 'em all right once he's gone," Douglas reminded them.

"Yes, but we'd like to fix *him*, too," said William. "Think of all the things he's done, an' we've done nothin' back at all."

"How *can* we do anything?" said Ginger again.

"Oh, shut up sayin' that," snapped William, who was feeling rather irritable.

"Well," said Douglas pacifically, "the only thing to do is to jus' watch an' find out what he's doin' each day. We may be able to think of a way before he goes."

They received this suggestion without enthusiasm.

"I don't see how we can find out what he's doin' or what we can do if we do," said William, "but I don't see that we can do anything else, so we'll jus' do that."

They decided to reconnoitre in couples and to report at a meeting the next evening. William's plan was to follow Mrs. Lane about in the village and listen to her conversation (fortunately she was an extremely garrulous lady), while Ginger's was to hide in the hedge that bordered the Lanes' garden and to which Uncle Charlie's hearty booming voice might be expected to reach. Douglas accompanied William, and Henry, Ginger. Their scheme was successful, though they need not really have resorted to it, as Uncle Charlie was himself proudly publishing his plans throughout the village. He had written to the headmaster of the school which the Outlaws and the Hubert Laneites attended and offered to give a Talk on his Travels. Uncle Charlie loved the limelight—even such doubtful limelight as is afforded by a school Talk—and he was anxious to extend his popularity beyond Hubert and his circle. He had broadcast religiously the fact that he was "fond of children", his hostess continued to refer to him as a "great boy" or a "boy at heart", but the fact remained that few boys, beyond Hubert's immediate circle, had responded to his charm. And he liked to think of himself as a sort of modern Pied Piper, followed wherever he went by a crowd of admiring boys.

The Outlaws, of course, he had not tried to charm—he considered that he'd got a lot of innocent boyish fun out of the Outlaws *v*. Laneites feud—but he had distinct suspicions that they wouldn't have responded even if he had tried to charm them. And so he had written to the headmaster offering to give a Talk on his Travels. Uncle Charlie had travelled, but not as extensively as he gave people to understand. He was, indeed, himself, somewhat vague as to where he had been and where he hadn't, because he found it just as easy to talk about places he hadn't been to as about places he had been to. Sometimes he read up guide-books, but quite often he didn't even bother to do that.

The headmaster, who had met Uncle Charlie, wasn't really keen on the idea of the Travel Talk, but agreed to have it on the day before the last day of term, as it would solve the eternal problem of what to do with the boys on that day. He wrote to Uncle Charlie, thanking him for his kind offer and saying that he'd be glad if he could see his way to give the address on the day before the last day of term. Uncle Charlie was beside himself with excitement. He saw his fame spreading . . . spreading . . . saw himself delivering his famous Travel Talk at every public school in the country, saw himself regarded as one of the greatest educators of the day. ("Oh, yes I understand what boys like. I'm still a boy at heart, you know.") He paid a surreptitious visit to the nearest town and bought a few new books of travel in order to extend his repertoire. So exuberant was he at the prospect that he climbed up into the tree again and emptied another bucket of water upon the Outlaws (he was, after all, a man of somewhat limited ideas), and managed to scatter a little of it on to each of them.

Then he had a further inspiration. He would make more than a mere Talk of his Travels. He would make an Event. He sent for more books of travel. He went up to London and paid a visit to a theatrical costumier. Finally he unfolded his plan to the Hubert Laneites. He had decided that, as his talk ranged from country to country, Hubert and his friends should appear in turn on the platform, wearing the appropriate costume of the particular country about which he was speaking. They would change in a room behind the platform and come forward at pre-arranged signs. The idea seized hold of Uncle Charlie with such intensity that he could talk and think of nothing else. He saw himself as a Cochran staging the world's largest "show". His travels became more extensive each minute. Guide-books arrived by every post. He paid another, and yet another, visit to the theatrical costumiers and gave reckless orders. He held daily rehearsals with Hubert and his friends. In the intervals he found time to keep up his reputation for "boyishness" by dropping lighted squibs on to the Outlaws from the tree that overhung the road and sending a box of chocolates to William by post, every one of which he had filled with cayenne pepper.

"A regular Peter Pan, isn't he?" said Mrs. Lane delightedly, when he described these tricks to her. To the Outlaws the most maddening part of it was that they could devise no method of retaliation. Even William's usually ready flow of ideas seemed to have stopped.

They were nervy and irritable and could do nothing but bandy useless reproaches.

"Can't you think of *anythin'*?" demanded Ginger bitterly.

"Think of somethin' yourself," snapped William.

When the news of the Talk reached them, however, some of their irritability departed. They became thoughtful.

"We might do somethin' about that," said William slowly.

\*     \*     \*

The day of the Talk arrived. To the masters it was a heaven-sent respite in which they could get on with correcting their exam. papers. The youngest master, to his intense disgust, was detailed to be "in charge" over the assembly. He considered that he could do this quite well if he sat in the next class-room with the door open and corrected his papers there.

The boys surged into the big hall, prepared to be bored, but not really minding, because the holidays were so near. And, anyway, whatever it was, it was better than lessons. No one noticed that the Outlaws were absent.

The Outlaws were, in fact, just carrying a suit-case through the school yard.

The Hubert Laneites were putting on their first costumes in the "green room" behind the stage. Hubert was struggling into an Esquimaux costume, Bertie Franks was considering a Chinese costume, and wondering which way up it went on, and the others were morosely doing the same with the costumes of various other nationalities. On the wall behind them hung an elaborate list of the order of their appearances and the sequence of changes. On the floor was a dress-hamper

overflowing with national costumes. The Hubert
Laneites looked dejected and resentful. Uncle Charlie
had rehearsed them without mercy for days, and they
were sick of the whole affair. Moreover, they felt that
whatever glory came of it would belong to Uncle Charlie
and not to them. Uncle Charlie would make sure of that.
They turned suddenly to see William and the Outlaws
standing in the doorway. William's expression was
unmistakably pacific.

"He told me to tell you it's been put off till this
afternoon," he said, "so he says you'd better go now.
He says he's expecting a big box of cream buns from
London, an' it'll be at Hadley station now, an' if you like
to go an' fetch it you can."

The faces of the Hubert Laneites brightened. They
loved cream buns. They were delighted at the respite
from the "dressing-up", whose zest had finally departed
in the course of Uncle Charlie's rehearsals. They pushed
and struggled with each other in the doorway, each
trying to get out first, then ran as fast as they could
(which wasn't very fast) towards the spot where the
Hadley bus stopped.

The Outlaws breathed a sigh of relief. That disposed
of *them* for a bit. They couldn't possibly be back before
the end of the morning. Left in possession of the field,
the Outlaws bundled Uncle Charlie's carefully chosen
costumes into the dress-basket and opened the battered
suit-case that Ginger was carrying. From that they took
out William's much-worn Red Indian costume, a hearth-
rug, an old bathing gown of Ethel's, a pyjama suit, a lace
curtain that William had rescued from the "rag bag",
and an old top hat of Ginger's father's that was one of
their cherished possessions. These, with a ragged
tablecloth, a broken basket plant-pot, some burnt cork,

and what was left of Ethel's lipstick after the measles rash, comprised their properties. William put on the Red Indian costume and the top hat, and had barely got his face corked with an "imperial" and upturned moustache, when the little bell, that was Uncle Charlie's signal, sounded in the other room.

William stepped out of the green room on to the platform. Screens had been put along the back of the platform, leaving a small aperture at which the "actor" was to appear. Uncle Charlie stood at a reading-desk at the front of the platform well towards one side. Fortunately for the Outlaws, Uncle Charlie had considered it more artistic to screen himself off.

"You see, boys," he had said, "I don't want you to look at me. I want you just to hear my voice describing these wonderful countries I've visited and then look at the native (ha! ha!) who will magically appear between the screens. Just listen to my voice and watch the space between the screens at the back, that's all. Now the first country I visited was Japan." He rang his little bell. "Here is a native of Japan. . . . A little Japanese. . . . Give-a-chap-an-easy-one, eh what?" William in Red Indian costume and top hat appeared in the aperture. The school rocked with delight. Uncle Charlie, taking their mirth as a tribute to his wit, smiled modestly and hastily re-arranged his notes.

His notes had been prepared somewhat sketchily and were not very easy to follow. One or two of them had got out of order, and what made it specially difficult was the fact that he had actually visited so few of the places he described that he really wouldn't have known if his papers had got mixed up. He could, however, utilise the few moments of applause that would greet the appearance of the "native" in sorting out the pages and

WILLIAM APPEARED, IN A TOP HAT AND RED INDIAN COSTUME.

making sure that they were consecutive. Fortunately, he
needn't look round to see that the "natives" were all
right. He'd left them such a detailed time-table of their
order of changings and appearances that they couldn't
possibly make a mistake. Moreover, the little chestnut
about Give-a-chap-an-easy-one had gone down very

well. He'd make a little joke each time and that would prolong the interval.

He read a short and extremely dull account of Lapland, which he had never seen, describing one or two

THE SCHOOL ROCKED WITH DELIGHT.

very unconvincing adventures, which had never happened, and ended: "Now I'll show you a native of Lapland dressed exactly like the people I myself saw there." He rang his little bell and added: "Laplander doesn't mean he laps land, you know. He laps milk just like anyone else." A roar of delight greeted this joke and he smiled again—his most complacent smile—as he set to work to arrange his papers. He couldn't know, of course, that Ginger had appeared in the aperture dressed in Ethel's bathing dress, his nose reddened, the wicker plant-pot on his head. So great was the applause that the youngest master appeared at the doorway of his class-room, but just at that moment Ginger had disappeared behind the screen. The master glanced at Uncle Charlie. His face still wore its complacent grin. The old fool must have made some joke, and the boys were always ready to laugh at anything or nothing at the end of term.

He returned to his class-room and decided not to come out again, whatever happened. He'd got as many corrections as anyone else, he told himself bitterly, and he didn't see why he should waste his time listening to that old ass's bletherings. Riotous roars of laughter continued to reach him as Henry appeared in a hearth-rug with a saucepan on his head, as a Chinaman, and Douglas in the lace curtain with his school cap on his head, as a Turk.

Uncle Charlie was not really surprised at the burst of continued applause and laughter that greeted the joke with which he always introduced the "native". He had often thought that his wit was not appreciated as it should be by his immediate circle. These boys, at any rate, seemed to have a true appreciation of it. And so the "lecture" rambled on, to an accompaniment of wild hilarity, as the Outlaws appeared in costumes that grew more and more daring, Douglas and Henry having dashed home to fetch tea-cosies, tablecloths, aprons, plant-pots, shoe-blacking, and even the counterpane from Ginger's bed. It was while William (as a native of Russia) stood between the screens, his nose reddened and the rest of his face blacked, wrapped in Ginger's counterpane and wearing a tea-cosy for a hat, that the headmaster, attracted by sounds of mirth that seemed incompatible with anything in the way of Travel Talk he had ever heard, appeared suddenly in the doorway.

Uncle Charlie's complacent smirk grew yet more complacent. "You see what I am," it seemed to say, "just a great boy. I don't know what I've done to amuse these kids so much . . . though I must admit some of my jokes were pretty good." He was beginning to say something of this sort, when he saw that the head-master's grim gaze was fixed, not on him, but on the native of Russia, who stood trembling in his counter-pane and tea-cosy. Uncle Charlie, looking round and seeing him for the first time, gave a start of surprise.

"What's the meaning of this?" he said.

But no one was listening to him. Everyone was listen-ing to the headmaster.

\*  \*  \*

Half an hour later the Outlaws walked slowly homeward. They were sadder if not wiser boys.

"An' we've had all this awful time over it," said William, "an' it's done no good at all really. He'll prob'ly be worse than ever 'cause he heard all what Ole Markie said to us an' . . . "

But he stopped suddenly. A cab was coming down the road towards the station, and in it was Uncle Charlie, who was making his escape before the story should be all over the village and making it none too soon. He scowled at the Outlaws then leant forward, shaking his fist.

The Outlaws stood and watched the cab in silence for a moment before they broke into a dance of triumph in the middle of the road.

# Chapter 9

# Pensions for Boys

William walked down the road, whistling his loud untuneful whistle and kicking a suitably sized stone from side to side. He wasn't going anywhere in particular, so it didn't matter when he got there. Even if he had been going anywhere in particular it wouldn't have made any difference. William considered it a waste of time to walk straight along a road. If there weren't stones to kick, there were ditches and hedges to investigate, trees to climb. . . .

He was feeling unusually light-hearted. School was to break up next week, and four golden weeks of leisure stretched before him. He was already forming plans for it. The first day he and the Outlaws would make a tent in the wood. They'd train Jumble to catch rabbits for them, and cook them over a fire. They'd—the sound of a deep chuckle reached him and he looked round, startled. He had seen the figure of an old man hobbling down the road in front of him, but old men did not interest him, and he had not taken much notice of it. Surely the chuckle could not have come from that bent hobbling figure. He quickened his pace. Yes, there it was again. The old man was chuckling to himself as he walked along the road. William was interested and decided to follow him. He turned into a lane and made his way, still chuckling, towards a small cottage at the end of it.

William followed. The door stood open, and a girl was leaning idly against the doorpost. The old man chuckled at her and went inside.

"Who is he?" said William curiously.

"Him?" said the girl. "That's grandpa. It's the day he gets his Old Age Pension. He's always cock-a-hoop the day he gets his Old Age Pension."

"What's that?" demanded William.

"What's what?"

"His Old Age—what you said."

"Old Age Pension? Fancy you not knowing that! He gets ten shillings a week. Goes to his head the day he gets it."

"Ten——" The magnitude of the sum took William's breath away. "Who gives it him?"

"The government."

"What for? What's he done?"

"Nothing. They give it him jus' 'cause he's old."

"Well, there's lots of other old people," said William. "Why do they pick him out?"

"They don't, stupid," said the girl. "They give it to all old people."

"*What?*" said William, incredulously. "Do you mean to say that they give all old people all over the country ten shillin's a week?"

"Course they do," said the girl. "Didn't you know that? Where've you been living all these years?"

William's amazement was gradually giving place to indignation.

"Well," he said. "I call that jolly mean. Why, ole people simply don't know what to *do* with money. They don't like sweets, nor games, nor anythin' int'restin'. They don't like fireworks, nor circuses, nor animals, nor air-guns, nor mouth organs nor——" he paused for breath, then went on. "Jus' fancy *anyone* wastin' money, givin' it to old people! What does he do with it, anyway?"

"I dunno," said the girl indifferently. "Comes home cock-a-hoop with it, that's all I know."

"There isn't *anythin'* he can do with it," said William, "an' ole man like that."

"He buys tobacco with it."

"Tobacco!" echoed William scornfully. "There's nothin' int'restin' about tobacco. Anyway, he can't spend ten shillin's on tobacco. Ten—shillin's—a—week," he repeated slowly. "Seems awful to me givin' ten shillin's a week away to ole people. I've never had as much as ten shillin's in one week in all my life that I can remember an'——"

But the girl had tired of the subject and had gone indoors, closing the door behind her.

William gazed at the door for some moments in silence, then, muttering indignantly: "Ten—shillin's—a—week," he turned and walked slowly down the lane. This time he did not whistle or kick stones. He was staggering beneath the weight of a crushing injustice. That the government should each week lavish the munificent sum of ten shillings upon a section of the community notoriously incapable of appreciating any of the proper uses of money—the monstrous unfairness of it almost stunned him. He didn't, he told himself, grudge the money to old people. But what was done for one should be done for all. He felt amazed that this glaring anomaly should have been allowed to exist for so long. It was certainly time it was stopped.

His face was stern and set when he joined his Outlaws in the old barn. They saw at once that he had a grievance, but, though he began to expound it with all

the eloquence at his command, it was some time before
they realised what it was. As in the case of a good many
orators, the more eloquent he became, the more difficult it was to know what he was talking about.

"Jus' *think* of it . . . ten shillin's . . . ten shillin's a
*week* . . . and jus' think what *we* could do with it, ten
whole *shillin's* every week . . . an' why should they
have it an' not us? It's not fair . . . I'm s'prised the King
lets it go on. I shouldn't mind if we *all* had it . . . an' I
don't see why we shun't all have it . . . an' if everyone
can't have it then no one oughter . . . it's only
fair . . ."

"Yes, but what is it?" demanded Ginger patiently.

"I keep tellin' you," said William. "Why don't you
*listen*? I keep tellin' you that the government gives it to
'em for nothin' at all. They don't have to do anythin' at
all for it. It's jus' giv'n 'em. An' we don't get anythin'.
Not a penny. They get ten shillin's a *week*—an' we don't
get anythin'. An' we work all day long, goin' to school
an' doin' sums an' suchlike, an' they do nothin' at all but
just sit about, an' yet they get ten shillin's a week."

"Who gets ten shillin's a week?" said Douglas.

"Ole people. I keep *tellin'* you. They get ten shillin's a
week for doin' nothin'. If anyone oughter get it, it's us.
We work all day long goin' to school an' suchlike an'—
well, it's not fair."

"I know about it," said Henry. "It's called the Old
Age Pension."

"I don't care what it's called," said William. "It's
jolly unfair, an' if you're goin' to start stickin' up for
it . . ."

"I'm not," said Henry hastily. "I'm not stickin' up
for it. I'm only tellin' you what it's called."

"Well, I don't care what it's called," said William.

"It's jolly unfair." He considered a moment then said, "Can any ole person get it?"

"I think so," said Henry. "I know a man that used to be our gardener does. He jus' goes into the post office an' asks for it an' they give it him."

William looked more thoughtful still.

"Well," he said at last, "we can have a jolly good try, anyway."

The next evening William, wearing an old hat of his father's, a large grey beard that had figured in all the family theatricals ever since he could remember, and an overcoat of Robert's, entered the post office. Ginger, Douglas, and Henry waited outside.

William approached the counter, and, after clearing his throat, spoke in a high unsteady voice supposed to be suggestive of extreme old age.

"I've come for my ten shillin's," he said.

The post-mistress gazed at him in blank astonishment.

"Your—what?" she said.

"My Old Age Pension," quavered William. "I've only jus' come to live here, so I'll be comin' for my ten shillin's now every week. I . . . "

But he got no further, for the post-mistress leant over the counter and delivered a box on the ear that dislodged both beard and hat, and sent William himself staggering into the road.

"You saucy little hound!' said the post-mistress indignantly. "Get out of here and if you come in again . . . "

But William had already joined his friends outside. He was rubbing his ear ruefully. The beard hung precariously from the end of his tie.

"That's no good," he said. "She wouldn't even wait for me to explain. I was going to tell her I was ninety, but

"YOU SAUCY LITTLE HOUND!" CRIED THE POST-MISTRESS.
"GET OUT OF HERE!"

my birth certificate had got burnt up by mistake in a fire,
but she wouldn't listen. She's a very bad-tempered
woman. I'm sorry for real old people what go there for
their money if that's the way she goes on at 'em all."

"I s'pose we'll jus' have to give it up," said Ginger.

He spoke sadly, for the prospect of earning ten shillings a week by the simple process of going into a post
office and asking for it had been a pleasant one.

"No, I don't see why we should," said William firmly. "I don't think that anythin' as unfair as that oughter be allowed to go on. People in history got unfair things put right, so I don't see why we shun't. I bet we're as good as people in hist'ry any day. They stopped people havin' slaves, an'—an'"—he turned to Henry. "What else did they stop?"

Henry considered for a moment.

"They stopped children workin'," he said at last.

"*What?*" exploded William. "Stopped children *workin'*. Stopped *children* workin'. Well, what else do we do, I'd like to know? We work all day long. We're fairly wore out with work. Why, when I count up how many sums I've had to do in my life——"

"I don't mean that sort of workin'," said Henry. "They stopped 'em workin' in mills an' down mines an' up chimneys an' that sort of thing."

"What cheek!" said William indignantly. "I'd a jolly sight rather work in a mill or up a chimney than in school. I'd've *liked* workin' in chimneys an' things. It'd've been a jolly sight more interestin' than doin' sums an' Latin an' suchlike. D'you mean to say children used to be let work in mills an' mines an chimneys?"

"Yes."

"Well, why couldn't they have left us alone instead of comin' interferin' with us? I've always wanted to go down mines an' up chimneys. You have little lamps an' go down in a lift an' get black all over an' there's ponies there. It mus' be jolly nice. An' goin' up chimneys mus' be almost as much fun. An' instead of lettin' us go on enjoyin' ourselves they come interferin' an' make us go to school instead. *School!* Huh! It's jus' my luck to live in the time when we go to school instead of mills an' mines an' chimneys an' things. I always seem to live in the wrong time in history. There's hardly a single time in history I wouldn't sooner live in than the one I do. I——"

"Well, about these pensions," said Ginger gently, leading him back to the subject in hand. "How're we goin' to get it put right?"

"Well, how *did* people get things put right?" said William. "I don't mean puttin' things *wrong* like stoppin' us goin' into mines and chimneys an' havin' a bit of fun." William was beginning to feel a sense of bitter personal injustice on this score. "I mean *really* puttin' things right, like slaves, though I bet slaves had a jolly sight better time than I have. When I think——"

"Yes," said Ginger hastily, knowing that William's eloquence must be stemmed in time or it couldn't be stemmed at all. "Well, let's think how to get this pension thing put right."

"I've got an aunt," said Henry slowly, "what was one of the people what got votes for women. There only used to be votes for men till this aunt of mine an' some others got it put right."

"What did they *do*?" said William.

"They did all sorts of things," said Henry. "I've often heard her talkin' about it. They chained themselves to railings."

"Why?" said William.

"I don't know, but they did. An' they got it in the end."

"How would chainin' themselves to railin's get it them?" demanded William with interest.

"I don't know, but it did."

"We could do that all right. At least, we could tie ourselves to a fence, but I don't see how that'd get it us. Still, we'll try everything."

"An' they went to prison an' wouldn't eat anythin' there."

"That's silly," said William. "I don't mind goin' to prison, but I'll jolly well eat anythin' I can get when I'm there. I never see any sense in not eatin'."

"An' they shouted out 'Votes for Women.'"

"All right, we'll shout out 'Pensions for Boys.'"

"Won't we get it for girls, too?" demanded Douglas.

"No, we jolly well won't. Girls don't know what to do with money. They only waste it. We'll jus' get it for us. Pensions for Boys."

"They had banners an' things."

"Well, so will we. What else did they do?"

"I dunno, but she's comin' to tea to-morrow, so I can ask her."

The next day they met in the old barn to await Henry, who arrived soon afterwards, looking very important.

"I've found out a lot of the things they did," he said. "They went round the country makin' speeches about it. My aunt an' some others took a lorry round an' made speeches about it in the streets."

"We'll take a wheelbarrow," said William, "I can make jolly good speeches. Did people listen to 'em?"

"Yes, an' threw things at them."

"We'll throw things back if they start doin' that at us. I'm a jolly good thrower. What else did they do?"

"They shouted out 'Votes for Women' at public meetings same as I told you, an' they put bombs in churches an' set fire to things."

"Where did they get bombs?"

"I dunno. I expect fireworks'd do."

"We've not got any fireworks," said William. "We used them all up in November, an' you can't buy them this time of the year. Anyway, we couldn't even if you could, 'cause we haven't any money."

"We've gotter box of crackers left over from Christmas," said Ginger. "I bet that'd do."

"Did they get that thing they wanted?" said William.

"The vote? Yes, they got it all right."

"Well, I bet we get ours, too. It's a good thing we break up on Tuesday. It gives us all the holidays to get it put right in. An' we won't waste time either. We'll start to-morrow d'rectly after school."

After school William returned home and, with a dexterity born of long practice, managed to abstract the garden wheelbarrow while the gardener's back was turned. He trundled it along to the old barn, where the other three awaited him. Henry had brought his drum, Douglas his bow and arrow, and Ginger his pea-shooter. "It'll come in handy if people start throwin' things at us," he explained.

William surveyed the little band of reformers with pride.

"We oughter get it all right," he said. "I bet we can do all the things as well as those what's-their-names did them."

"What'll we do first?" said Ginger.

"I'll make a speech from the wheelbarrow first," said William. "I'd better do that while I'm fresh. Besides, I've been thinkin' out things to say an' I might forget 'em if I put it off too late."

They trundled the wheelbarrow down to the road and helped William on to it. Henry took up his position on one side with his drum and Ginger on the other with his pea-shooter. Douglas stood behind with his bow and arrow.

William looked up and down the empty road impatiently.

"Well, I can't wait here all day," he said, "an' I'll

forget what I was goin' to say if I don't start soon. Someone'll be sure to come along in a minute." He struck an eloquent attitude and began: "Ladies an' gentlemen, it's jolly unfair, an' we've all gotter work hard to get it put right. Why should they have it an' not us? That's what I want to know. An' ten *shillin's*! Ten shillin's a *week*! What do they do with it? Nothing, either. They can't. They're too old. It's wasted on 'em. They don't even like sweets—not any of the ones I've met. Jus' wasted on 'em. Wastin' hundreds an' hundreds of ten shillin'ses every week, while other people, what'd know what to do with it, haven't enough money to buy anythin' at all. I don't mind 'em havin' it. I keep sayin' that. Only if they have it *we* oughter have it, too. It's jolly unfair. We only had one pen'oth of bulls'-eyes all last week, an' sometimes, with people keepin' back money, what belongs to us, for windows an' things, we don't get any at all."

By this time the audience consisted of one small child, sucking a piece of rock, who seemed to have sprung up from nowhere. She stood in front of William, gazing at him dispassionately, holding the end of her rock with one hand, while her cheeks went in and out like small bellows with the action of sucking. William, who was tired of addressing the landscape, turned to her and flung out his arms eloquently.

"Well, *isn't* it jolly unfair?" he said. "Jus' think of it. Ten shillin's a week. Ten shillin's a week for doin' nothin', while we work an' work an' *work* day after day an' week after week' doin' Latin an' sums an' hist'ry an' stuff an' don't even get a penny for it."

He paused dramatically, and in the pause the small child removed her rock and said: "Be quiet, I'm trying to think."

"THEY GET TEN SHILLIN'S A WEEK FOR DOIN' NOTHIN',
WHILE WE WORK AN' WORK AN' WORK DAY AFTER DAY."

"*Think?*" echoed William indignantly. "What do you
want to think for? Anyway, if you want to think, you can
think about what I'm sayin'."

"I don't want to think about what you're sayin'," said
the small child. "You're not talkin' sense."

She replaced her piece of rock in her mouth with an air
of finality.

"Not——?" exploded William, hardly believing his
ears. "Not talking *sense*? *Me*? *Well*, I like that. Here I

am, tellin' you about this unfair thing that's happenin' all the time all over the country, an' you say I'm not talkin' sense. Don't you *want* ten shillin's a week?"

The small child removed her rock, said "No," and replaced it.

William stared at her for a moment in silence. Then, "What *do* you want?" he demanded sternly.

The small child removed her rock.

"I want to see a fairy," she said.

Sheer horror deprived William of the power of speech, but only for a moment.

"*Fairies!*" he exploded. "There aren't any. Hasn't anyone told you that yet? There *aren't* any."

"There are," said the small child, calmly.

"There aren't."

"There are."

"There aren't."

"There are."

It occurred to William that he was wandering from his subject.

"Now listen to me," he said. "About this ten shillin's business. They have it every week an' we oughter have it, too. It's only fair. That's what I say. It's only *fair*."

"I wish you wouldn't talk so loud," said the small child. "I'm tryin' to think."

"Well, go somewhere else an' think."

"No, you go somewhere else an' talk."

"No, I came here first."

"Well, you can go first then."

William was slightly nonplussed by this argument.

"What d'you want to think about?" he said, with reluctant curiosity.

"Fairies," said the small child.

William made a gesture of disgust and stepped down from his rostrum.

"S'not much good stayin' here," he said to his band, "talkin' to a loonie. *Fairies!*" he exploded again.

The road was still completely empty except for themselves, the small child, and an old man sitting at the door of his cottage in the distance, making passes at a fly with his ear-trumpet.

"Let's try somewhere else," suggested Ginger, and added: "There mus' be someone somewhere."

"No," said William, "I'm sick of talkin' with no one listenin' to me. Worse than no one listening, I mean. *Fairies!*" He threw a look of contempt at the small child who stood sucking her rock, staring blankly into space. "Come on," he continued, taking up the handles of the wheelbarrow and beginning to trundle it down the road. "What else did they do?"

"They put bombs in churches," said Henry.

"Well, we've got crackers, but it's no use doin' that till Sunday. Good thing it's Sunday to-morrow. What else did they do?"

"They called out 'Votes for Women' at public meetin's."

"What's a public meetin'?"

"I dunno . . . people meetin' in a public house, I 'spect."

"Well, let's go'n' see if there's anyone in the Red Lion."

There was a group of men at the bar. As the Outlaws opened the door someone made a joke that was, apparently, a good one, as the roars of laughter that greeted it quite drowned the Outlaws' piping chorus of "Pensions for Boys". But the publican saw three small boys on the threshold and advanced upon them threateningly. They backed apprehensively before him. He shook his fist at them.

"You come in here once more," he said, "an' I'll give you somethin' you won't forget in a hurry. D'you want me to lose my licence?"

Then he shut the door on them.

"What's his licence?" said William.

"It means temper," said Henry. "Well, he's jolly well lost it already."

Ginger put his mouth to the doorway and shouted daringly "Pensions for Boys", but that effort, too, was drowned by a roar of laughter from within.

The four Outlaws walked disconsolately away.

"Well, I dunno how it is," said William. "We're doin' all the same things they did, but we don't seem to be gettin' on very well."

"There's the crackers yet," Ginger reminded him.

"Yes, we'll try 'em to-morrow. Don't forget to bring 'em."

William's family and Ginger's often occupied the same pew in church, and on this occasion William and Ginger managed to get together—a proceeding that was generally out-manoeuvred by their families. The Litany had been chosen as the most suitable time for the demonstration, and, as soon as the rest of the family had buried their heads in their hands, Ginger took a cracker from its hiding-place under his coat, and, holding one end, handed the other to William.

"One . . . two . . . three . . . " whispered William.

They pulled.

The cracker came apart with a sudden "plup" that was drowned by the Vicar's high-pitched resonant voice. They tried again. The same thing happened. The third was no more successful.

"Don't fidget, William," whispered Mrs. Brown and Ginger's mother looked up from her prayer book and tweaked his sleeve.

"Haven't you another?" whispered William.

"No, I couldn't hide more'n three."

"Don't talk, William," said Mrs. Brown.

William stared dejectedly in front of him. He'd meant, by a daring piece of lawlessness, to startle the world into granting his just demand—and all he'd achieved was a mild reproof for fidgeting. Fate seemed to be against him in every way. Even the choir boy at whom he usually pulled faces wasn't there.

When they met in the afternoon, Ginger bore their reproaches with dignity.

"Well, I'm sorry," he said. "We'd had 'em since last Christmas, an' the pipe burst in the cupboard they were in, but they'd got quite dry again, an' I din't know their bang had got spoilt. Well, how *was* I to know? They *looked* all right. . . . Anyway we've done all they did an' now . . . "

"No, we haven't," said Henry. "She was talkin' about it again last night. They had a banner with 'Votes for Women' on, an' they walked to London with it."

"We could do that all right," said William.

"London's a jolly long way off," Ginger reminded him.

"Yes, but if we keep on walkin' we'll get to it. If you keep on walkin' you get anywhere. Anyway, we can start."

They agreed. They were as disinclined as William himself to abandon the enterprise in this unfinished state.

"We'd better begin makin' a banner," said Henry.

"What did you say they had on it?" demanded William.

"Votes for Women."

"Well, we'll have 'Pensions for Boys'."

"They made speeches on the way."

"I'll do that. I've not had a chance yet. No one's listened to me but that batty kid. I've thought out lots more things to say since then, too."

"When shall we start?"

"School breaks up on Tuesday morning. We'll start on Tuesday afternoon. We'll start the banner to-night."

The banner was, in the eyes of its makers, at any rate, an unqualified success. Douglas found the remnants of a sheet in his family's rag bag and cut a large square (which happened to contain three patches, but which was otherwise intact). William and Ginger inscribed the words PENSHUNS FOR BOYS in red paint that ran somewhat, but that was still more or less decipherable. Henry procured a broom handle and a box of tacks and nailed the banner on to the broom with his shoe. They hid it carefully in the old barn on Monday when they parted for the night.

"We'll go home for lunch after breakin' up," said William, "an' start d'rectly afterwards."

"We won't be back for tea," said Ginger. "It's miles an' miles an' miles to London."

"We may not be back for weeks," said Douglas.

"I bet they'll be all wond'rin' what's happened to us, when we're not back to-night. They make enough fuss if we're a minute late."

"The world'll be ringin' with our names by then," said William optimistically. "We may've got the lor passed by then. Ten shillin's a week! I wonder we've put up with it all these years. They oughter give us all the back ones—startin' from when we were born."

"It'd come to an awful lot," said Ginger. "I don't

suppose they've got so much. We'd better let 'em off that. But we won't come home till we've got the ten shillin's a week."

"No, we jolly well won't," agreed the others, with enthusiasm.

That evening William threw out cryptic hints to his family about the length of time that might elapse before they saw him again, and the place his name would occupy in the annals of fame, but they were so used to cryptic utterances from William that they took no notice of them.

Next morning the "breaking-up" took place without any untoward incident, and, directly after lunch, the four met again in the old barn. The banner looked even better than their memories of it. They gazed at it with gratification.

"I bet it'll give 'em all a bit of a fright in London," said William, "when they see it comin' along."

Douglas, who had recently had to write out the word "attention" fifty times, was slightly doubtful of the spelling "penshuns". Reasoning by analogy, he said that it ought to be "pentions", but the others overruled him.

"Course it's all right," said William, "p-e-n pen and s-h-u-n shun. Stands to reason."

The others agreed that it did, though, as Ginger added darkly: "You never know, with spelling."

Ginger had been put in charge of the provisions. He had brought a broken and discarded attaché-case of his brother's to carry them in and each of the four had contributed what they could. William had brought some apples, Henry some bulls'-eyes and a packet of ants' eggs (which, he said, must contain nourishment or goldfish could not live on them), Douglas some rock cakes into which the cook had forgotten to put baking powder, and which she had given to a beggar who had tasted one and left the others on the front doorstep, Ginger a tin of sardines, opened and half full.

They set off down the road, William carrying the banner, Henry his drum, Ginger the attaché-case (its sides were loose, and it had to be tied together with string) and his pea-shooter and Douglas his bow and arrow. Several people looked at them curiously, but no one spoke to them. When they had marched for about half an hour, William stopped.

"Let's have a rest," he said, and added: "I wonder how near London we are now. I bet we're almost there."

"I'm gettin' jolly hungry," said Douglas plaintively.

Ginger opened his attaché-case and surveyed the contents anxiously.

"We've got to eat it very gradual," he warned them. "There's not much, an' we don't want to die of hunger before we get to London. Ten shillin's a week won't be much good to us if we're dead of hunger."

"We jolly well won't die of hunger," said William. "Not if I know it."

"We might," said Douglas. "People in sieges do."

"Well, we aren't in a siege."

"I know, but it's the same in a way. They eat up all the food an' then they have to die of hunger or live on horse-flesh."

"We'll live on horse-flesh," said William. "There's plenty of horses about."

Ginger was still examining the contents of the case. A look of concern had come into his face. The sardine tin had overturned during the journey, and everything was swimming in sardine oil. Rock cakes, apples, bulls'-eyes and ants' eggs were soaked in it. He took out the apples, surreptitiously wiped them on his coat, and handed one each to William, Douglas and Henry.

William bit his, chewed thoughtfully for a second or two, then stopped.

"It tastes of sardine," he said.

"Well, it's a good taste, isn't it?" said Ginger. "There's nothing wrong with sardines."

"I know, but it's funny with apple."

Henry looked into the case.

"Everything's covered with sardine," he said. "My ants' eggs are ruined."

"Well, what's wrong with sardine?" said Ginger again, indignantly. "Anyone'd think sardines was poison by the way you're all goin' on. It's a jolly good taste. I bet in some countries they eat it with everythin' same as we do salt."

"It's all right with things it goes with," said Douglas, who had taken a tentative bite at a rock cake, "but it doesn't go with cake or apples or sweets. That's all I say."

"You're so jolly particular," said Ginger. "Grumblin' at everythin'. You'd better start eatin' horses straight away."

"I shan't be sorry when we do get to horses," said William, bitterly. "They won't taste of sardine, anyway. Why couldn't you have packed the stuff so that *everythin'* didn't taste of it? It's rotten with bulls'-eyes."

"All right. Do it yourself next time," said Ginger huffily.

"'S all very well sayin' that now, when everythin's *ruined*. Well, I'm goin' to start makin' a speech. Someone's sure to come along soon."

There was a convenient stile by the roadside on to which William mounted. Henry with his drum stood on one side of him, and Douglas with the flag and bow and arrow on the other. Ginger was tying up the attaché-case and muttering: "Some people'd be jolly well glad of sardine."

Across the road was a large building with "Wentworth School" on the gate. William examined it with interest.

" 'Spect they've broke up, same as we have," he said, "but if they've not we'll stay here till they come out, an' I bet we'll get a lot of them to join us. They can march to London with us. An' they can get some more food," he glanced sternly at Ginger, "some food what isn't soaked in sardine. Anyway, I'm goin' to start. I'll be practisin' on you till someone else comes along." He cleared his throat, struck an attitude and began: "Ladies an' gentlemen, we're marchin' to London because we want to get things put right. We want to have ten shillin's a week same as other people. We do a jolly sight more work for it an'——"

The doors of Wentworth School opened, and a trickle of schoolgirls began to emerge. William, who had never even contemplated the possibility of its being a girls' school, was slightly disconcerted, but he was beginning to enjoy his own eloquence, and was glad of any sort of an audience, so he continued:

"——an' we jolly well oughter get ten shillin's, too. Anyway, they just waste it, an' we could use it prop'ly. What I say is——"

A group of girls had gathered around them. A breeze fluttered the banner displaying the somewhat erratically printed letters.

" 'Penshuns for boys'," read out a long, thin girl with a long, thin nose and a long, thin plait, who was the centre of the group. "It's spelt wrong."

"I *told* you," said Douglas.

"It isn't," said William. "Anyway, there's lots of ways of spelling it. There is of most words."

"What's it mean, anyway?"

"Well," explained William, "I've only jus' found out about it, or I'd have got it stopped long ago. All ole men get ten shillin's a week jus' for doin' nothing, an' we work so hard we're almost wore out with workin'—I know I'm wore out every day with Latin an' sums an' suchlike—an' yet they don't give us a penny. Not a *penny*. So we're goin' to London to get it put right."

"How're you goin' to get it put right?" said a girl with a snub nose and red hair.

William considered this question for the first time.

"We're goin' to march into Parliament an' make a speech about it," he said.

"I bet you don't know where Parliament is."

"No, but we can find out, can't we? We'll go to the post office an' ask. They always know where places are at the post office. They have to 'cause of sending letters there."

The long, thin girl was still looking at the banner.

"Why've you got just boys on it?" she said. "Aren't you goin' to get it for girls, too?"

There was a pugnacious gleam in her eye. William hesitated for a moment, then decided to stand by his convictions.

"No," he said, "we're only gettin' it for boys."

The gleam in the long, thin girl's eye became still more pugnacious.

"Why?" she said.

"Well—girls've got enough money."

"Oh, no, they haven't," said the long, thin girl, "an' if you're goin' to have a pension, we are, too. Why should you have it an' not us?"

"I'm only gettin' it for boys," he said loftily. "If you want to get it for girls, you can. I'm not stoppin' you."

"We'll join up with you," said the long, thin girl.

"No, you won't," said William. "We don't want you. We don't want girls."

"An' why don't you want girls?" said the long, thin girl, with ominous distinction.

"We don't like 'em."

"An' why don't you like 'em?"

"We're as good as you any day," squeaked the girl with red hair, "or better. Better, I *should* say."

"Why don't you like 'em?" repeated the long, thin girl.

William's dislike of the long, thin girl had increased till it was a positive relief to give vent to it.

"'Cause they're soppy an' batty an' stuck-up an' stupid," he said. "'Cause they can't play fair or talk sense. 'Cause——"

The long, thin girl advanced upon him pugnaciously.

"Oh, that's what you think of girls, is it?"

"Yes, it is," said William.

"Well, you wait till I tell you what I think of boys. An'——"

She took another step towards William, which Ginger interpreted as a prelude to a personal attack. He slipped a pea into the pea-shooter and dexterously emitted it. It landed on the very end of the long, thin nose.

Suddenly all was confusion. The long, thin girl hurled herself upon William, and the others followed. They had no clear idea of what it was all about, but these boys had attacked their leader, and, after a morning in school, they were ready for anything—especially as they outnumbered the foe about five to one. They set upon them tooth and nail. William was grabbed by the neck, tripped up, his hair pulled, his face scratched, his head pummelled. He hit out wildly, but his enemies were like a swarm of gnats. Nimbly they evaded his blows and closed in on him again immediately, scratching, grabbing, pushing. Ginger, Henry and Douglas were also surrounded by a crowd of them. The enemy increased as more girls came out of school and joined the fray, several of them with hockey sticks. Two hockey sticks hit William simultaneously on either side of his head. Someone thrust a ruler into Ginger's eye. The business end of a geometrical compass was jabbed into Douglas's arm.

They were pushed back to the stile, over the stile into the field. William landed ignominiously, head foremost. The long, thin girl took up the attaché-case containing provisions and flung it after him. It fell open upon his face. He sat up and wiped bits of sardine out of his eye. The banner followed, hitting Henry in the chest and winding him.

The Outlaws got up slowly and collected what was left of their belongings. Ginger's pea-shooter, Henry's drum, and Douglas's bow and arrow were in the enemies' hands. The red-haired girl beat the drum derisively, and the long, thin girl sent out a pea that hit Douglas neatly on the side of his head.

"Come on," called the long, thin girl. "Come on. We're waiting for you."

The entire school appeared to have joined them, every member of it now armed with a hockey stick.

"Come on," they shouted. "We're ready for you."

William stood up, removed some ants' eggs from his mouth, and looked around with the air of a general surveying a campaign. A torn collar and a film of sardine oil over his face detracted somewhat from his dignity.

**WILLIAM SAT UP AND WIPED BITS OF SARDINE OUT OF HIS EYES.**

"We won't go back to the road," he said. "They're more like wild animals than human beings."

He looked around him again. A path led across the field to another stile.

"Come on," he said, "let's go that way. I bet we can find a path back to the road higher up."

"COME ON!" CALLED THE LONG, THIN GIRL. "WE'RE WAITING
FOR YOU."

"We've still got the banner, anyway, so we can go on
marchin' to London."

The cries from the girls over the stile became shriller
and more insulting.

"Don't take any notice of them," said William.
"Let's get on over the fields till we come to another

road. Then we can go on marchin' to London."

"We've got no food now," said Douglas disconsolately.

"I have," said William bitterly, "I've got sardine all over me. I don't think I shall ever taste anythin' but sardine again as long as I live."

"We'll have to beg, that's all," said Ginger. "I've often wanted to try beggin'."

"Or work our way, same as people do in books," said Henry.

"Or eat horses," said Douglas.

"I bet they'd taste of sardine if we did," said William. "Everythin' tastes of sardine. Anyway, I don't want to eat anythin'. I don't think I'll ever want to eat anythin' again."

They had reached the farther hedge now. A stile led over into another field. William stood on the stile and gazed about him.

"I bet that's a bull," he said, pointing to a sturdy, stocky animal that stood peacefully grazing in the middle of the field.

"It looks a tame one, anyway," said Ginger.

"Yes, they act tame till people get right up to them," said William, "then they turn savage."

They glanced back. The crowd of girls was still there. The hockey sticks seemed to have grown even more numerous. Shouts of derision and challenge still floated faintly across the field.

"It'll have to be the bull," said William. "P'raps it is a tame one. There mus' be *some* tame ones. Stands to reason. They can't *all* be wild. Same as people. Come on. We'll go very quietly, so as not to disturb it."

Slowly and fearfully they climbed down from the stile into the field and began to make their way across on tiptoe. The bull fixed one fiery eye on them, but continued to graze. In single file, on tiptoe, holding their breath, the Outlaws approached it, passed it, then heaved a sigh of relief.

"It *was* a tame one," said William. "I thought it was. I'm jolly good at bulls. Soon as I saw it I thought, that's a tame one, that is. I bet I could have managed it all right even if it'd been a savage one. I've often thought I'd like to be one of those people in Italy what fights bulls. They're called tor—something."

"Torpedoes," suggested Ginger.

"No, that's a kind of flower. No, these tor—something men don't care how savage a bull is—same as me. They jus' goes up to it—same as I would—an'——"

"Look out, it's comin'," whispered Douglas. They turned round. The bull was following them—quite slowly and calmly, but definitely following them. Two fiery eyes were now fixed on them.

"Don't run," whispered William. "They run after you if you do. All wild animals do. Jus' go on walkin' an'——"

At this moment a gust of wind came and spread out the banner that Henry was still carrying, displaying the words "Penshuns for Boys". Either the sentiment or the lettering seemed suddenly to infuriate the bull.

There was an angry bellow, a sudden thud of hoofs, and the Outlaws fled in panic towards the nearest hedge. Fortunately Henry had flung away his banner to make his flight easier, and the bull fastened angrily upon it, goring it, tossing it, stamping on it. The Outlaws scrambled through the hedge and then stood panting for breath. They found themselves in a small and very neat garden. They could hear the snorting of the bull on the other side of the hedge, and backed fearfully away from it.

"What are you doing in my garden, boys?"

They wheeled round to see an elderly lady standing at an open window. They were too breathless to answer. William pointed to the field and she nodded understandingly.

"Oh, I see, the bull. How silly of you to go into the field! There's a notice up, or ought to be. Perhaps it's at the other stile. It ought to be at both, of course. Well, come in and rest."

She vanished from the window and soon appeared at the open doorway.

"Come in," she said.

Panting, dishevelled, they entered the small, spotless cottage parlour.

"I don't think I know you," she said. "You don't live here, do you?"

William found breath to reply "No."

"What are you doing here, then?"

"We're walking to London."

"You've a long way to go yet."

"Have we?" said William, anxiously. "I thought we mus' be nearly there."

"You're fifty miles off, at least."

"*Fif*——? Gosh! We mus' have only come about six miles. I thought we'd come fifty. I *feel*'s if I'd come fifty."

The lady looked at him dispassionately.

"You *look* as if you'd come much more than fifty," she said. "What are you going to do in London?"

"I'm goin' to make a speech to Parliament," said William.

The lady did not seem at all surprised by this announcement.

"What about?" she said.

"Pensions for boys."

"What?" she said.

He explained the situation, and she listened with interest and sympathy.

"I'm very much afraid it's no use," she said, gently, when he had finished. "You see, I was one of them, too. A suffragette, I mean. I marched to London and made speeches at street corners and shouted 'Votes for Women' all over the place, and—well, we'd never have got it if it hadn't been for the war. It was the war that made them give it us, not anything we did."

"Oh," said William. "You mean we'd better wait till the next war?"

"I'd wait quite till then," said the lady.

"Well, I mus' say," admitted William, "we've not got very far yet, an' we've been workin' at it hard ever since last week. Those *girls*!" he ended in a tone of deep disgust.

"I know," sighed the lady. "The men were just as bad to us. So unchivalrous."

William sighed too.

"It seems jolly unfair," he said.

"I quite agree with you," said the lady. "I remember just what it felt like." She took out a purse. "I know this isn't much, but it's better than nothing, and it may just help to cheer you up."

She handed half a crown to each of them. Their faces brightened. It was certainly better than nothing.

"Thanks *awfully*," they said gratefully.

The lady went to the window.

"It's a good thing you got out of that field when you did," she said.

They looked out. The bull was still busy with their banner. The broom handle was now a mass of splinters.

PENSHUNS hung crookedly from one horn and BOYS was a sort of garter half-way up one leg.

"I must certainly get them to put up a notice at the other stile," said the lady.

"Well, I don't see how we could go on, anyway," said William, "without a banner or food or a drum or anything."

"You've been very unfortunate," said the lady.

"Yes, we jolly well have—except for the half-crown," said William. "Thanks awfully for that. Well, we'd better be gettin' home now."

"Won't you stay and have some tea?" said the lady. "I'm afraid I've only got a very plain tea, but"—as a sudden idea struck her—"I could open a tin of sardines."

William blanched.

"No, thanks," he said hastily. "I mean, we'd better get home to tea. Thanks awfully for the half-crown and for being so decent."

"That's quite all right," said the lady. "I know so well how you feel. I've been through it all myself. . . . If you go out of the front door you can get straight home by the main road without meeting girls or bulls or anything else. Perhaps you'll come to tea some other time?"

They thanked her and took their leave, walking slowly down the road.

"Well, we'll jus' have to wait for the nex' war," said William. "It's evidently no good tryin' to do anythin' till then."

At the heart of each was a secret relief. The magnitude of the task they had so lightly undertaken had been oppressing them heavily during the last half hour or so.

"It was jolly decent of her to give us those half-crowns," said Douglas.

"Yes," said Ginger, "it makes ten shillin's altogether. It's a jolly sight better than nothin'. An' I'm jolly hungry."

"So am I," said William. "I thought I'd never be hungry again, 'specially when she began to talk about sardines, but I b'lieve I am now. We'll just about be back in time for tea if we hurry."

They quickened their pace, each clasping his half a crown tightly in his hand. . . .

# Chapter 10

# A Spot of Heroism

William sat alone in the railway carriage and watched telegraph poles, cows, and trees fly past the window. He was mildly interested in the sight and amused himself by pretending that it was the train that was stationary and the surrounding countryside that was moving.

Mrs. Brown had gone into a nursing-home for a slight operation, and, in order to relieve the domestic strain, William was being sent to stay with an old school friend of hers, who lived at a small seaside resort called Sea Beach.

He was enjoying the journey. He always enjoyed journeys. He enjoyed the motion and the change from the ordinary routine of life. They had a generally exhilarating effect on him, and he could, of course, enliven them by pretending that he was anyone going anywhere.

Since the journey began he had pretended that he was a spy travelling disguised through an enemy country (none of the other people in the carriage suspected him), a general on his way to the war (the other people in the carriage were his staff), and a circus man travelling with his show (the large man with the long nose was an elephant and the woman in the black satin coat was a performing seal).

All the other passengers had got out at various

stations, and now William was alone, pretending to be a wizard, who, by a wave of his wand, made trees, fields, telegraph posts skip to his bidding.

After a few minutes he tired of this; he was growing slightly bored. Suddenly his eye lit on the notice: "To stop the train, pull down the chain."

He stretched out his hand to it, then read: "Penalty for improper use, £5", and, after a hasty mental calculation that assessed his entire capital at the sum of one shilling and sixpence halfpenny, put his hand down again.

But the fascination of it was more than he could resist. He fingered the chain, and imagined himself pulling it. He wondered if it really worked and, if it worked, how it worked. It probably put on a sort of brake. There wouldn't be any harm in just pulling it a tiny bit. That would only just make the train go a little bit more slowly. No one would even notice it.

He pulled the chain an infinitesimal fraction.

Nothing happened.

He pulled it a little harder.

Still nothing happened.

He pulled it harder still. There was a sudden screaming of brakes, and the train drew to an abrupt standstill.

William crouched in his corner of the carriage, frozen with horror. Perhaps, he thought desperately, if he sat quite still and didn't move or breathe, they wouldn't know who'd done it.

The guard came running down by the side of the train. As he approached William's carriage, an elderly, red-faced, military-looking gentleman leant out of the next window, and gasped: "Guard, guard! You're in the nick of time"; then poured out an incoherent story about a man who had demanded money from him, and was just raising his stick to brain him when the train stopped.

"Then, of course, he jumped and escaped," he ended. "Look! There he is!"

The figure of a large but nimble man could be seen disappearing across a field on the other side of the train. Immediately outside the carriage was the stick that he had evidently thrown away in his flight.

"Just in time, guard," panted the military-looking man, mopping his brow. "Another minute, and——"

William heaved a sigh of relief. No one would now know that it was he who had pulled the chain.

"But you didn't pull the chain, sir," the guard was saying.

"No, the brute was standing right over me, so that I couldn't move. He——"

"The chain was pulled from this carriage," went on the guard, moving towards William, who sat in his corner, frozen by horror once more, trying to efface himself against the carriage back.

The guard stood and looked at him for a few seconds in silence, then he said:

"That was smart work of yours, nipper. I suppose, sir," he went on, turning to the military-looking man, "he heard this fellow threatening you and pulled the chain."

William, after a few seconds' complete bewilderment, clutched gratefully at this heaven-sent deliverance.

The military-looking man shook hands with him, thanked him effusively, and gave him a ten shilling note. The other passengers came up and crowded round him, wringing his hand and congratulating him. An old lady gave him a peppermint drop. A little girl produced an autograph album and asked for his signature.

THE PASSENGERS CROWDED ROUND AND CONGRATULATED
HIM.

William, though still somewhat bewildered, assumed
an air of modest heroism.

Finally, the guard, having taken all particulars of his
adventure from the military-looking man, sent everyone
back to their carriages, and the train started once more
on its way.

William, alone in his carriage, felt at first merely a

great relief at his providential rescue from ignominy.
Then gradually the imaginary scene became more and
more real. He saw himself starting up at the sound of a
fierce altercation from the next carriage, then coming to
a sudden decision and dashing to the chain. He sat for
the rest of the journey smiling modestly to himself,
bathed in a roseate glow of heroism.

His hostess, Mrs. Beacon, met him at the station. She
was a large, placid woman who, William decided at
once, would probably be amenable but uninteresting.
He hoped that she would realise that he was a hero. He
meant to lose no time in telling her the story.

But it wasn't even necessary to tell it to her, for it
turned out that several of the passengers were coming to
Sea Beach, and they crowded round William once more,
recounting his exploit to his hostess and congratulating
him.

William's modest but heroic smile intensified. He
depreciated his exploit with airy gestures.

"Oh, it was nothin'," he said; "it jus' sort o' seemed
the only thing to do. It was nothin' at all really."

But Sea Beach didn't appear to think it was nothing at
all. There had been a complete dearth of local news for
several months, and it seized on William with avidity.

Its local paper sent a reporter to interview him and
printed his portrait on its first page under the heading:
Our Boy Hero. People pointed him out to each other as
he walked along the promenade, wearing his modest but
heroic smile.

His hostess prepared specially appetising food for him
in order to fortify his nerves after the ordeal through
which she supposed them to have passed.

For a whole week William revelled in the limelight,
then quite suddenly, as it seemed to him, it was gone. A

fresh edition of the local paper had come out announcing that a leading inhabitant had won a bowling-match at Morton-on-the-Water, where he was spending his holidays, and that the Mayor's daughter was preparing to swim the Channel.

Moreover, Miss Arabella Love, a well-known musical comedy actress, had arrived at Sea Beach, and in this welter of new sensations William's exploit was completely forgotten.

William himself, as is usual in such cases, was the last person to realise this. He continued to walk along the promenade, wearing his modest but heroic smile, and it was some time before the fact dawned upon him that no one was watching him or talking about him. They were all watching and talking about Miss Arabella Love—a platinum blonde with a ravishing smile and an apparently inexhaustible wardrobe.

William ceased to depreciate the heroism of his exploit. One cannot indeed depreciate something that is never mentioned. He began to recount his exploit vaingloriously and with many additions. He described how a ferocious ruffian had suddenly begun to threaten him in a railway carriage and how, after a tremendous tussle, he had managed to overpower him and pull the communication-cord.

No one but his contemporaries, however, would listen to him, and his contemporaries, after listening to him, would derisively recount similar exploits of their own. Even his hostess no longer prepared him appetising dishes but began to give him cold beef and rice pudding.

William stopped talking about his train exploit and became very thoughtful. He had tasted the limelight, found it good, and, like Oliver Twist, he wanted more, but he definitely and reluctantly came to the conclusion

that, as far as the limelight went, his train adventure was
dead.

The only thing to do was to cut his losses and start
afresh.

He felt all the bitterness natural to one who has
tackled a ferocious ruffian alone and unaided in a railway carriage (he did really remember it like that by now)
without winning any lasting gratitude or kudos from his
fellows, but he wasn't going to own himself beaten. A
hero he was, and a hero he would continue to be, and, if
the train exploit didn't stand good any more, he'd find
something else.

The world was full of opportunities of heroism. You'd
only got to read the papers to see that. Why, he might
rescue someone from drowning. . . .

The thought of that encouraged him, and he began to
haunt the little beach at the fashionable bathing hours.

Miss Arabella Love was always there, dressed in the
latest bathing-model, parading to and fro on the beach
or paddling in the foam, surrounded by her crowd of
admirers. The reporter from the local paper followed
her about with his camera and interviewed her at regular
intervals on the burning questions of the day. (She
thought the League of Nations was "just too cute for
words".)

William sat in the shadow of the rocks and watched
this scene morosely. Even if he rescued someone from
drowning, would it eclipse this horrible woman with the
horrible name?

Then the brilliant idea struck him. He'd save *her* from
drowning. That surely would give him all the limelight
he could desire.

So far her "swimming" had been of a somewhat
primitive nature. She had merely splashed about at the

edge of the sea, but she'd surely try to swim properly some time or other, and then——

William watched and waited, hanging about on the beach in his bathing-suit, ready for all emergencies.

And, as everything is supposed to come tó him who waits, so to William there came a day when Miss Arabella Love lingered on the beach after most of her circle had gone in to lunch and, as if suddenly weary of posing and paddling, struck out into the open sea.

To William's disappointment, she seemed a fairly good swimmer, but he knew that even good swimmers occasionally get into difficulties, so he continued to watch hopefully from the shore.

Miss Arabella Love was, as a matter of fact, a very good swimmer, and was just learning the "Dolphin Roll". It is not, as practised by a beginner at any rate, a graceful stroke, and so the actress had waited till the coast was clear before she tried it.

Having got well out to sea, she began to practise. She floundered and plunged, and finally disappeared from view.

To William, watching her every movement, it seemed that his desire was at last granted. Miss Arabella Love was in difficulties. His heart leapt exultantly as he struck out from the shore.

He had had no experience in rescuing drowning people, but he thought that it would be easy enough. You just got hold of them and swam back to shore with them.

Miss Love was further out than he had realised, and he was somewhat breathless when he reached her. She was coming to the surface after a particularly strenuous "Dolphin Roll", when she found herself violently clutched at by a small boy.

Miss Arabella Love knew all about life-saving as applied to frantic drowning persons. She freed his hands, ducked him till he was practically unconscious, then swam with him back to the beach.

The news had spread, a crowd had gathered, and the reporter ran up with his camera. A cheer rose as the actress flung her burden upon the sand, and began to pump vigorously at his arms. Finally she said, "He'll be all right now," and, still kneeling by his side, posed for a few more photographs.

&ast; &ast; &ast;

Consciousness gradually returned to William. He had been ducked and pummelled ruthlessly, but, being of a robust constitution, had survived it. He sat up on the beach and looked about him. He looked at the sea, then at Miss Love, who stood over him, watching him solicitously. Then he heaved a deep sigh of satisfaction.

He'd rescued her. He must have done or she wouldn't be here. His gaze passed on to the attendant crowd and to the photographer, and he assumed his modest but heroic smile.

A tall, thin man stepped forward.

"Well, my boy, aren't you going to thank your rescuer?"

The modest heroic smile died from William's lips.

"My what?" he said hoarsely.

"This lady here," said the man sternly. "Miss Arabella Love. She rescued you from drowning, didn't she?"

"No, she didn't," said William indignantly. "I rescued her."

A roar of laughter answered him.

"But I did," he protested fiercely. "I tell you, I did. I

"SHE DIDN'T RESCUE ME FROM DROWNING," SAID WILLIAM.
"I RESCUED HER. SHE STRUGGLED SOMETHING TERRIBLE."

saw her out there drownin', an' I went out an' brought
her back. She struggled with me something terrible, but
I brought her back all right."

Another roar of laughter greeted this statement.

"Poor little chap!" said an old lady pityingly. "It's
affected his brain."

"Come, come, my boy," said the tall, thin man
gravely. "A joke's a joke, but that's a very poor one.
Thank the lady like a gentleman."

"But I *did* rescue her," William repeated wildly.

"You've all made a mistake. I saw her drownin' an' I swam out to her an'——"

At this point Mrs. Beacon arrived breathless, having received an exaggerated report of the incident from a friend who said that she had seen Miss Arabella Love wading ashore with William's body in her arms. She was relieved to find him still alive.

"Oh, William!" she panted. "I do wish you'd be more careful."

"But I was; I didn't," said William desperately. "They won't listen to me. It was me that did it. She was——"

"Poor little chap!" said the kind old lady again. "He's delirious. No wonder, considering he's just been at death's door, so to speak. I'd get him home and to bed, my dear, if I were you. Give him something hot to drink."

Mrs. Beacon led William away, still loudly and passionately denying his rescue, while Miss Arabella Love, wearing almost exactly the expression of modest heroism that William had so reluctantly discarded, stood in a little circle of admirers and described to the reporter her exact sensation when she felt the frantic clutch of the drowning boy.

\* \* \*

The full horror of the situation dawned upon William the next day when, opening the local paper, he saw a large and very flattering photograph of Miss Arabella Love, as the rescuer, and beneath it a small and very unflattering one of himself, as the rescued.

There followed a detailed account of the affair, described by the actress, and a comment on the folly of small boys who venture out of their depth, thus occasioning unnecessary trouble to everyone concerned, ending with a graceful compliment to "our distinguished and highly accomplished visitor".

William went about sunk deep in gloom. So far from being a hero he was now in the ignominious position of having been rescued—he, William—and by a woman with a name like Arabella Love.

To make matters worse, his rescuer adopted a proprietary attitude towards him, patting his head and flashing her ravishing smile at him whenever they met, quite undeterred by his scowls.

He promised himself grimly to let her drown next time, but the promise failed to yield him much comfort.

The worst part of it all was that Mrs. Beacon, thinking that his parents would be interested in the incident, had sent a cutting from the local paper to his home. The news would be all over the village by now. All his friends—and what was more important—his enemies—would have heard of it.

He, who had meant to return home as the hero of the train incident, would have to return to the pitiful rôle of the boy who had been rescued from drowning by Miss Arabella Love. And he couldn't do anything about it. There was only a week before he had to go home, and one couldn't do anything in a week.

Or could one?

His incurable optimism rose to answer the question. One could and one must. William was not the boy to submit tamely to fate. He was a hero, and he must, by some means or other, win back his heroic status.

A brief survey of the situation told him that life-saving was his only hope. He must save someone else from drowning, leaving no doubt in this case as to who was the rescuer, and who was rescued. If he could only do this, he would not only reclaim his position as hero, but also throw strong doubt upon Miss Arabella Love's pretensions to having saved him.

He began to hang about the beach again, wearing his bathing-costume, waiting for his services to be required, watching all swimmers, children and adults, with a stern and anxious eye.

The days passed with no result, however, and William continued to fill the ignominious position of "The Boy whom Miss Arabella Love had Rescued".

The last day arrived. Moodily, almost despondently (for even William's optimism had its limits), he wandered to the end of the wooden jetty that ran for some distance out to sea, in order to brood in solitude.

The jetty was deserted except for a large black dog of the Labrador species, who greeted William as a long-lost brother, and began to gambol in puppy fashion round his feet.

Even that failed to raise William's spirits, until, as he gazed down at it, an idea suddenly occurred to him. He looked at the shore. A fair number of people were there—among them, he noticed, the reporter from the local paper.

He went to the edge of the jetty, the dog accompanying him. Then, with a deft movement of his foot, he pushed the dog over the edge, and, flinging up his arms, dived in after it.

He soon found it, held on to it fast, and eventually reached land with it.

Luckily the people on the beach had seen the occurrence. A cheer went up and the reporter took a photograph. William, remembering the success of his modest demeanour over the train incident, merely smiled a deprecating smile and walked homeward.

He said nothing to his hostess. He meant her to

A CHEER WENT UP, AND THE REPORTER TOOK A PHOTOGRAPH.

remember later that he had said nothing to her. He saw her in imagination reading the glowing account of the rescue in the local press—it was fortunate that to-morrow was the day the local paper came out—and saying: "And he never even mentioned it to anyone. He just came home as if he'd been bathing as usual, and he never said a word to me about saving that dog's life."

The story would travel round the little seaside resort. "You remember that boy who saved the dog's life so pluckily? Well, he never even *mentioned* it when he got home." People would then recall the train exploit. "It was the same boy, you know, who tackled that ruffian in the train so bravely, and was so modest about it."

He was to start home by the first train the next morning. Mrs. Beacon prepared an early breakfast for him, but he ate it absently, glancing round as if in search of something.

"The paper not come yet?" he said.

"No, dear," said Mrs. Beacon. "It won't come till after you're gone. Why do you want the paper?"

"Oh, nothing," said William modestly, but he assured himself the news would be even more effective if it arrived after his departure. It would still further emphasise his modesty. ("He actually went home without mentioning it.")

At the station he had just time to buy a paper as the train steamed out. He leant back in his seat, a complacent smile on his lips. He'd show it to all his friends. His reputation as a hero would be made for life. Slowly he opened the page.

Yes, there it was—a picture of himself and the dog side by side. But when his eyes turned to the letterpress the smile died from his lips.

"DOG RESCUES SMALL BOY.

"A half-grown pup belonging to Miss Arabella Love to-day rescued from drowning the same small boy whom Miss Arabella Love herself rescued only a few days ago. We must . . ."

But William read no more.

THE END